THE

BRIGANDS

OF

PALESTRA;

OR,

TWO GALLANT HEARTS.

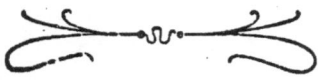

By

E. Harcourt Burrage.

THE BRIGANDS OF PALESTRA;

OR,

Two Gallant Hearts.

CHAPTER I.

OUTSIDE THE ITALIAN INN—PAPITA AND LUIJI—THE SHAM GARCON.

ABOUT fifteen miles north-east of the historic mountain, Vesuvius, stands the village of Palestra, an out of the way place, of which the world knows very little.

The ordinary tourist never visits it; indeed, for several years not an Englishman had set foot in the place prior to the opening of our story—a brilliant noon in early spring, when two men appeared at the door of the only hostelry in the place, and asked if they could dine there. Two lazy, blackbearded-fellows were lying against the wall, apparently sleeping. They heard the query addressed to the landlord, who was standing just inside the doorway, and one of them just unclosed his eyelids to look at the visitors.

The other made no movement whatever.

"Dinner, my lords?" replied the host, answering, as he had been addressed, in Italian. "Aye! and a rare one, too, if you have the money to pay for it."

"We can pay for all we have," was the brief reply.

"Then enter, my lords, and dine."

The two young men, handsome types of the Britisher, passed through the doorway, and were heard to follow the landlord to a room at the back of the inn.

As soon as the sound of their footsteps died away one of the men sat up, and the other sleepily opened his eyes.

"Heard you that?" said he who had risen. "Two Englishmen who speak of money as if it were dirt. They go and dine with Vampa, and do not even so much as ask what the cost will be."

"It is their way," said the other.

"They must have a lot of money about them, Papita."

"Perhaps, Luiji; but who can tell?"

"It can be found out," said Luiji, with a significant glance.

"Bah!" returned Papita; "such fledgings would not be worth the killing."

"Killing—no; but there is ransom. Varsanta has been sighing to replenish his coffers. Here is the chance. He will reward us well if we put two fat young Englishmen into his power."

"Again, perhaps," said Papita; "he is not always grateful. Do you

remember the old Spaniard we put into his clutches ?
What did he give us ?—blows."

"Ay ! but we were in error then, Papita. He was
not a nobleman, as we thought, but a travelling
quack. He had nothing about him but half-a-
dozen coins and a packet of his infernal powders."

"Well !   Your plan, Luiji ?"

"It is to go to Varsanta and tell him that two
rich Englishmen, who can dine without so much
as saying, 'What is your charge?' are to be captured and held to ransom, if he will but give us a
share."

"Well, go and make your bargain. I will remain
here and see what can be found out of their
concerns, for I care not again to risk troubling
Varsanta to capture a son of the fiend travelling
with physic."

Luiji rose up and strode away, and Papita watched
him as he wended his way in the direction of a line
fo rugged hills bearing north.

Then, as he was lost to view, Papita got up,
yawned, stretched his arms, and entered the
inn.

There was no bar, as we have in this country,
but at the far end of a low-built, dimly-lighted room
was a counter, on which stood sundry bottles and
glasses, under the care of an ill-favoured woman of
fifty or so.

"Signora Vampa !" said Papita, "where is your
husband ?"

"He is looking to the strangers," she answered ;
"for that lazy boy, Beppo, of ours is out somewhere
skulking in the sunshine."

"By the saints ! then I will be garcon to-day," said
Papita.

"You lazybones!" replied Signora Vampa. "What possesses you to seek work? Art gone mad?"

"No, I have reformed," was the light reply. "Behold in me a new man. Ah! here is Vampa."

If Signora Vampa was ill-favoured, she was well matched by her husband.

It was not so much a matter of features, for in his youth he must have been good-looking.

It was the repulsive expression of his face that stamped the man.

Evil passions, and a disposition possibly soured by the life of a needy man, had helped to make him what he was.

"A murrain light on that boy of ours!" he said "When there is anything to do he is not to be found."

"There is one who will fill his place," said Signora Vampa, with a shrill laugh, as she pointed at Papita.

"I have no money to pay for a garcon," returned Vampa, sourly.

"I ask for nothing," said Papita. "I will wait on these strangers and trust to their generosity. In their own country they pay for everything, even if they only ask the name of a street through which they are passing."

"But you are such an ill-favoured-looking dog," said Vampa; "you carry thief and brigand on your face, and in every rag about you."

"Give me one of the signora's aprons," said Papita, "and a napkin to carry on my arm. Then off with my hat—so, and my hair brushed back—thus, and there I am! Who dares to say I do not make a good garcon?"

But though a white apron and a napkin do much

towards making a man look like a respectable waiter, Papita was not particularly improved by them.

Vampa was still doubtful.

"Such a hang-dog, cut-throat face!" he said.

"Not when smoothed out," urged Papita, in no way offended by these left-handed compliments. "Oh! I can be olive-oil itself at a pinch. Si, signors, what can I serve you with? Command me—your servant. I am here to obey."

There was a marvellous change in the look of the ruffian as he mimicked the manner and speech of a cringing servant.

Again the signora laughed, and Vampa smiled dryly.

"You may pass," he said, "if you play your part thoroughly. Put down your knife, and wash that dingy face of yours; then you will do. When the host waits at table the charge must be moderate; but when we keep servants, why, then those who eat and drink under this roof must pay."

"I am ready," said Papita, with a bow. "What can I do to please their lordships?"

"They want a flask of wine—the red seal," said Vampa. "The best. They will have no other. Wife, get me two of your choicest glasses and a tray. We shall make enough out of these free-handed young fools to live for months to come."

A minute later Papita, with his cringing air fully developed, entered the room where the two young strangers were sitting.

It was a low-pitched apartment of plain stone walls, and with one long, narrow window at the end.

The furniture consisted of a heavy table, two

rude settees, one on each side of a fireless hearth, and half-a-dozen smoke-begrimed, moth-eaten chairs.

The Englishmen sat at the end of the table, looking out of the window, which commanded a view of the stable-yard at the back of the house.

There was not a family resemblance between them, yet they were somewhat alike, as friends are apt to become when they have spent years together.

Both were tall, well set up, and handsome, athletic fellows, such as can be found by the score at our colleges and public schools.

They were about the same age, too—something between eighteen and twenty-one.

The faces of both were beardless.

One was touching up a sketch in a worn pocket-book as Papita entered and with burlesque serenity placed a tray with the wine and glasses on the table near them.

"My lords—the wine," he said.

"Oh! hang this lord business," said he with the sketch-book. "We are not lords, my good fellow, but simple citizens of the British Isles."

"Your pardon, signors," said Papita. "I did not mean to offend. I am your servant."

"Very good. Uncork the wine, and when dinner is ready bring it in."

Papita went on playing his part to perfection, and backed out of the room, bowing half-a-dozen times ere he got to the door. When he got there he bent to the very floor, straightened himself, and then vanished.

"Confound the fellow!" said the visitor who had not previously spoken; "he's like a comic character in opera bouffe."

"For all that, Percy," replied the other, "he's a murderous-looking ruffian."

"You think so, Will?"

"I am certain of it. He can bow, and smile, and cringe; but he could not squeeze the devil out of his eyes."

"Shall I help you to wine?"

"Do, there's a good fellow."

For the present it will suffice for us to state that Percy Winter and Will Gordon were travelling for pleasure.

Percy had ample means at his command, his father being a rich man; but Will Gordon, although not absolutely poor, had very little to spare.

He was what he called studying for an artist, and he certainly had some talent; but he was not cut out by nature for a life in the studio.

A life of adventure was more in his line.

He and Percy had been schoolfellows together, and had read the stories of travellers with the gusto of youth.

Many a time they had expressed a longing to share great perils together, and in the enthusiasm of boyhood mapped out a cruise "when they were big enough" to cope with men.

And that enthusiasm was in them still. In sober truth they were travelling together out of the beaten route with the hope of "something turning up."

Something, and more than something in the ordinary sense of the word, was about to turn up.

Their longing for adventure would shortly be fully gratified.

CHAPTER II.

BEPPO THE PRODIGAL.

EVENING came, and the glory of an Italian sunset was on the rugged scene the travellers looked on from the door of the inn.

To the left was the open country, with the hills in a golden group. To the right were the scattered time-worn houses of the village, covered with ivies and creepers, and with picturesque groups of Italian peasants at the doors.

Percy and Will were smoking briar-root pipes, lazily delighted with all things around them, and occasionally breaking into the easy conversation of those who are contented.

They were the objects of great interest to the villagers, who, however, held aloof from them, save a few of the most daring children, who came near, to stare at them for a minute and then run away.

One, a hero among his fellows, distinguished himself by calling out, "Englise!" which was looked upon as a daring attack on the strangers.

"Amusing little beggars!" said Will. "I would like to sketch some of them if they would stand still for awhile."

fully gratified.

stand still—no pay. Here comes a likely subject."

He pointed to a boy about fourteen, strolling into the village from the country—a ragged, sunburnt, handsome urchin, barefooted, with curling hair about his face, and a lock or two peeping through the crown of a too-well ventilated hat.

Altogether a very picturesque little fellow.

On seeing the strangers he stared at them until his two big black eyes were painfully prominent in his face ; but he came straight towards them, with his hands behind his back, without halting or showing any intention of running away.

Indeed, it was apparent that he was bound for the inn, and his identity may at once be revealed It was Beppo, the careless, idle son of Vampa the host.

"He has stepped out of a canvas by Murillo," said Will, enthusiastically.

"And here is our host stepping out to say something unpleasant to him," remarked Percy.

Vampa came out with a very ominous-looking pliant stick in his hand, at the sight of which Beppo pulled up short.

By his face he recognised a familiar but not very pleasant acquaintance.

"Beppo—varlet !" hissed Vampa, "where have you been to-day ?"

Beppo offered no reply. Probably he knew that giving a full statement of his movements would not mend matters.

He cast a quick glance at his father, then at the strangers, as if pleading for them to intercede.

The two friends were amused. The angry father and the prodigal son made a splendid picture.

" Dog !" hissed Vampa ; "ungrateful son. See— two lords here to-day, in need of being waited on and you—away idling."

" I met Varsanta," replied Beppo, "and he sent me with a message to the castle. Would you have me disobey *him* ?"

" Lies—lies !" cried Vampa, furiously ; "it is always Varsanta."

He sprang forward with the intention of seizing the boy, who did not budge.

Having a hiding to take he no doubt thought that it would be better to get it over without any waste of time. But Will, advancing, intervened.

" Don't thrash the little fellow," he said. " We have done very well without him."

It may be here explained that both our friends spoke the Italian language, which we translate for the benefit of the reader.

" He is disobedient," said Vampa ; "he must be beaten."

" No—no," replied Will, pushing the old man back ; " not on my account."

" I will beat him for other things neglected."

" No—you really must not. It isn't a fair fight."

" What !" cried Vampa, " shall I not do as I like with my own son ?"

" No, I'll be hanged," replied Will, " if I stand by and see him cut about with that murderous cane. Why, it would split the skin upon his bones."

" Don't think of it, old man," said Percy. " We shall not allow it."

" Shall I be mocked by him—laughed at ?"

" You are not to beat him now, at any rate."

Vampa looked at them with knitted brows, and slowly lowered his weapon.

"If you, my ords, wish it, he shall be let alone,' he said, with a swallowing action of his throat.

"We will ransom him," said Percy, laughing. "Another bottle of that good wine won't hurt, and you may have one for yourself. Put both down in the bill."

"My lords, you are royally generous," replied Vampa, bowing.

He turned on his heel and entered the inn.

Beppo, who had stood quite still, all eyes and ears, ran up to the friends, and, before they could guess his intention, had kissed a hand of each.

"Ask me, and I will die for you," he cried.

"Italian for much obliged, that is," said Percy. "Well, young shaver, who is this friend of yours who sends you on errands that last all day?"

"Varsanta," said the boy, with flashing eyes.

"Then he is no myth? You really were sent?"

"Varsanta says, 'Go,' and I fly. Who here *dare* disobey him?"

"Really," said Percy, "he seems to be a man of importance. Who is he—lord of the manor?"

Beppo shook his head.

"We have no lords here," he answered.

"Who is he, then. Policeman—beadle—"

"He is—Varsanta," said Beppo, "and do you beware of him."

And then, before they could put another question to the boy, he was gone.

"What do you make of that, Percy?" asked Will.

"Oh! Varsanta is the bully of the neighbourhood," replied Percy. "They seem rather short of gendarmes here. I enquired of our humble garcon, Papita, if there was such a thing in the village, and what do you think was his answer?"

" Can't guess."

" Sometimes—that was his answer. They some-times get a gendarme here. It is good. Between his visits this Varsanta, whoever he may be, appears to be cock of the walk. There goes the last rays of the sun—the beauty of the land has fled. Let us go in to our room."

" What shall we do to-morrow ?" asked Will.

" Explore those hills," answered Percy, with a yawn, as they entered the inn. " I am told that there are some old castles, once the homes of power-ful noblemen, hidden away there."

" But we shall want a guide."

" Suppose we engage the prodigal Beppo? He will be out of harm's way with us."

" Agreed."

On entering the room which they had previously occupied they found Papita in the act of placing their wine on the table.

They told him of their intended excursion on the morrow, and bade him send Beppo to them to be engaged as guide.

Keeping up his mock serenity, the ruffian left the room, and after a considerable delay came back again.

" Beppo, my lords—signors," he said, " has gone to bed, weary with idling about, but the good Vampa will see that he is ready for you on the morrow."

" Perhaps we can do without a guide," said Will carelessly.

" Signor," replied Papita, " it is not safe—so many paths—so many places in which to get lost, and one must have a guide to the castles. They are so hidden away."

"Well, then, we will start after breakfast on the morrow," said Percy Winter.

"The more I see of that fellow," said Will, when the effusive Papita had retired, "the less I like him."

"We need not bother about liking or disliking a garcon," replied Percy, easily. "Fill up—this wine won't hurt you. It is the best stuff I've tasted since we put foot into this country."

The friends sat discussing their bottle of wine until it was quite dark. A lamp was brought in, but they said they did not want it, and expressed a desire to be shown to their room.

Vampa himself lighted them upstairs to a chamber with two beds in it.

It was a huge apartment, and there was little else in it. Vampa apologised for the poverty of the place.

"We are poor," he said, "and get no patronage—but, my lords—we have done our best."

"Thanks," said Percy, "there is nothing to complain of. We don't expect the luxuries of a first-class London Hotel. Call us at six, please, and have breakfast ready by seven."

Vampa promised their orders should be obeyed, bowed himself out of the room, and left the friends to themselves.

"There are bolts to the door," said Will, "and we may as well use them."

"I don't think it matters," yawned Percy; "the people seem honest enough."

"You never can tell," said Will, as he drew the bolts.

They were tired, having walked a considerable distance in the early morning, and ten minutes later both were in bed and asleep.

An hour afterwards a panel in the door was drawn noiselessly aside, and a man, without shoes upon his feet, crept into the room.

After listening intently, and assuring himself by their heavy breathing that the visitors were asleep, he carefully felt his way to the chairs on which Percy and Will had placed their clothes.

With singular dexterity he singled out their coats, and with the garments tucked under his arm he left as noiselessly as he had entered.

The panel closed, and with his spoil he hastened downstairs to the room where the visitors had been regaling themselves.

It was Papita who had performed this stealthy feat, and with an exultant face he presented himself to three persons assembled in the room.

Vampa and Luiji were two of them, and the other was a well-built, handsome man, with a saturnine expression of face—it was Varsanta, the brigand.

That all three were afraid of him was made manifest by the way in which they kept their eyes upon him, watching his every movement.

He took the coats from Papita, carelessly tossed them upon the table, and with a deft hand turned out the pockets one by one.

He replaced everything, even some loose money, and betrayed no interest until he came to a small pocket-book belonging to Percy Winter.

This he opened, and carefully scanned some of the pencilled entries therein.

The reading was agreeable to him, for a pleased smile gradually spread over his face.

" Luiji," he said, " you have done well."

This appeared to be praise indeed, for the face of Luiji flushed to a deep red with the pleasure he felt.

"Put these things **exactly** where they were before," said Varsanta, as he returned the pocket-book, "and do not touch a single thing. I shall be prepared for the young English bloods to-morrow. You know where to bring them to?"

"The secret road to your castle—yes," replied Papita.

"Let there be no bungling in the job," said Varsanta, "or woe betide. Now, Vampa, good friend, bring me a bottle of wine and some cigars. By-and-bye I will pay for them with the Englishmen's money."

CHAPTER III.

PAPITA AS GUIDE—THE CASTLE PASS—TREACHERY—A PLUCKY FIGHT.

"I AM sorry, my lords," said Vampa, "but Beppo cannot be your guide. The young scoundrel has taken advantage of your intervention yesterday, and has again gone out for an idle day."

"Ah! well, we must do without a guide," said Percy. The two friends had breakfasted and were just ready to start. Each carried in his hand a short alpenstock. "Without a guide —impossible!" said Vampa; "you would lose your way."

"Then we will find it again," replied Will.

"But you will see nothing of the old deserted castles hid among the hills. You would only waste your time looking for them," urged Vampa.

It was the castles Will wished to sketch, and not to see them would make a blank of the day.

"Who will be our guide, then?" asked Will, im- inpatiently.

"Papita—my servant," replied Vampa. "He knows every stone of the mountains."

"Such an ill-looking dog!" said Will. "I have no desire for his company."

"Oh! bother his looks," said Percy. "We need not trouble ourselves about him. It is Papita or no one."

"It is so," returned Vampa.

"Then Papita be it," said Percy, laughing. "Come," he added, as their host left the room, "do not look so glum. What is this man to you or me?"

"Nothing," answered Will; "and yet I feel when he is near as if a bird of ill-omen were hovering about us."

"The same old story, Will."

"Ah! you may smile; but I am not the victim of a petty superstition. In my family there runs a strange gift—that of having presentiments that seldom fail to come true. Mischief will come of that fellow's company."

"What can the hound do? Surely, Will, we have no cause to be *afraid* of him?"

"No, it is not that; nor can I tell you what it is? Never mind. I hear him coming. Let him be our guide."

Papita now put in an appearance, washed and

brushed up for the occasion ; but nothing could take away the villainous general appearance of the fellow.

There are some men who seem to have been cast in a mould for a statue of villainy, and Papita was one of them.

Though there was nothing but his looks to give cause for apprehension.

He had no visible weapon, not even the knife familiar to every Italian peasant.

" Signors," he said, " I am at your service."

In his right hand he carried a leathern wallet with a strap, and as he spoke he threw the latter across his shoulder.

The wallet contained wine and food for the day.

On leaving the inn Percy and Will saw that the whole village seemed to be interested in their going.

Men, women, and children were all about, but they kept their distance, and did nothing but stare.

"Travellers are scarce, I should say," said Percy.

" So should I," replied Will.

Papita strode on about a dozen yards ahead, and, when he did not forget himself, he was humbler than ever.

But now and then he would straighten up and roll along with an insolent swagger, very much at variance with his demeanor as a garcon.

Will marked it, and he liked him none the more ; but he made no comment on it to his companion.

It would seem foolish to offer a further objection to the rascal as a guide.

The level land was rough, for the road was ill-kept, and the country on either side only here and there showed any signs of being cultivated.

Such agricultural work as had been done was of the rudest description.

Not a soul was to be seen working on patches the of cultivated soil. Perhaps it was one of the numerous saint days, and a public holiday.

The distance to the base of the first mountain did not seem far, but the clear atmosphere was deceptive, and a good hour was spent in getting to it.

Papita said nothing all the way. Unlike the general guide, he was not intrusive, but now he paused to point out the route.

"Signors," he said, "we have to take the narrow path that winds to the north. It is a rough way, and a little rest will do you no harm."

"Get along man," said Will, tartly; "we are not in the lazy dog line. When we wish to rest we will tell you."

Papita cast a quick, angry glance at him, and with a muttered anathema on all "Englishmen with legs of iron," set out again.

Up the narrow way they went, and speedily found themselves amidst a chaotic arrangement of broken rocks—piled up around in the most fantastic form—with huge precipices and deep gulches here and there.

The path, as it was called, was only faintly indicated, and in some places it disappeared.

Only an experienced man, well versed in the country, could have easily found it again.

Papita was not at all troubled. He went on like a man who could have walked it blindfold, and so far his value as a guide was evident.

"We could not have got on without the fellow," said Percy, in a low tone.

"Well, we shall see how we get on with him," replied Will, dryly. "I see no signs of castles hereabouts."

They had now come to a spot where the path, clearer than it had been hitherto, wound round the base of a precipice, and in and out large boulders of stone, which formed excellent hiding-places for a concealed foe.

But our young travellers had no thought of such a thing in existence ; and when Will, finding one of his bootlaces loose, stopped to tighten it, Percy went on with Papita.

A few steps of the winding way took them out of the sight of Will, and Papita, casting a quick glance behind him, thrust his fingers into his mouth, and sent forth a shrill whistle.

"Hear the echoes, signor ?" he said, hurriedly.

Percy confounded the echoes, and turned to look for Will. The next moment two men sprang from behind the rocks, and, with his treacherous guide, threw themselves upon him.

He was dashed violently to the ground and half stunned, but did not entirely lose his wits.

Turning over on his back he made a desperate effort to release himself from their grasp, but his arms and legs were held in an iron grip.

"Silence ! you English dog," hissed Papita, drawing a knife from under his clothing, "or you die."

"Clear out, Will !" shouted Percy. "Don't come here. Brigands !"

It was a generous effort to save his friend, and, but for his value in the way of ransom, he would have paid the penalty of his daring with his life.

Will heard the cry; but, disregarding the warning, came clambering up to the aid of his friend.

But now Varsanta, with half a score of men at his heels, came pouring down upon the hapless Percy.

Some carried ropes, with which they quickly bound his limbs, and proceeded to drag him up the pass.

Will turned the corner in time to see what was being done, and valiantly dashed at the brigands, who, headed by Varsanta, barred his way.

In an instant he found himself in a whirlpool of ferocious men, who fought and cursed, but at the same time, obeying the voice of their leader, endeavoured to avoid doing him any bodily harm.

Two of the ruffians were felled by his alpenstock, and for a time they could do nothing but endeavour to collect their scattered wits.

Then the alpenstock was wrenched from him, and in true British fashion he fought with his fists, dealing out blows that brought blood from their noses, and made them howl with pain and rage.

But numbers prevailed, and at last down he went with half-a-dozen men upon him

They fairly spreadeagled him on the ground, and had him at their mercy exhausted and helpless.

"You dogs—you curs!" he said, between his teeth. "This is a scurvy trick, which you shall dearly repent of."

Varsanta, who had done nothing but look on and give directions to the men, now came up close to the prisoner.

CHAPTER IV.

VAMPA RECEIVES SOME FRESH GUESTS—GOOD TIMES FOR VAMPA—WHERE BRITISH PLUCK COMES IN.

YOU had better keep cool, my friend," said Varsanta. "It will be the better for you."

"Let me go!" replied Will, "or it will be the worse for you."

"Bind him and bring him along," said Varsanta; "he will be quieter by-and-bye."

Will made another effort to resist, but human strength and endurance have a limit, even with the strongest, and in a few moments he was as helpless as his friend.

"Drag him by the heels!" said Varsanta. "Having given us so much trouble he deserves it."

The panting men with fiendish glee hastened to obey, and Will saw that Papita was one who was most eager for the work.

They tied a rope round his ankles, and, as boys drag a sledge up a toboggan-slide, so they remorselessly drew him over the rugged ground up the mountain side. He held his head up while he could, but soon he began to tire, and presently it sank upon the ground. Then came the dreadful agony of blow after blow as they dragged him over the rough stones.

It was beyond the power of man to endure, and ere long his senses yielded, and he entered into the darkness of insensibilty.

It was late in the afternoon of the day of Percy and Will's capture by the brigands when three more strangers entered the village of Palestra. They did not, like their predecessors, come on foot, but riding on mules.

First let us give their names—Mr. Ribstone Pipping, Jane his wife, and Coriolanus, their son.

Mr. Pipping was a man under the average height, thick-set, smooth-faced, and dogged-looking.

Jane, his spouse, was also under the average height, and more than thick set. She was " round-set," being very stout. Her face expressed good temper, of the British matron order.

Of Coriolanus it need only be said at present that he was a discontented cub of thirteen, a spoilt child, and, in contrast to his parents, tall for his age, but lean. They were all three very tired, in fact, completely fagged out, and Mrs. Pipping was rolling in her saddle as if she had partaken of too much liquid refreshment.

But it was not so. She was fatigued.

" Now I wonder what sort of a crib this is ?" said Ribstone Pipping, looking about him.

" It doesn't matter," replied his wife, " so long as we've come to where we can rest and get something to eat and drink."

" But it *does* matter," said Ribstone Pipping. " A man like me has a right to have everything comfortable. I can pay for it."

" Why did we come fooling round here ?" asked Coriolanus. " Wasn't we better at home ?"

" It's the duty for rich English people to travel," returned his father, " They owe it—to—to—foreigners ; and look here, young fellow, don't you talk to your parents about fooling around when everything is being done for you—more than you've a right to expect."

By this time the mules had by sheer instinct brought the party to the open door and then halted. Behind them had gathered all the little boys and girls, and two or three idle adults of the village.

"Hallo! this looks something like a pub—ahem! INN," said Ribstone Pipping; "and I suppose this chap coming out is the landlord!"

It was indeed Vampa, who was a little bit staggered by the arrival of this second batch of strangers; but he came out bowing, and also managed to screw up a smile.

"Do you speak English?" asked Pipping.

"A leetle, signor," replied Vampa.

"That's good news," said Ribstone Pipping, "for I'm blessed if any of us can get hold of your confounded language, not even my boy Coriolanus, who's had a little fortune spent on schooling that's no good to him."

"I wasn't sent to the right schools," grumbled Coriolanus.

"Why, you—"

"Now don't you begin at each other," groaned Mrs. Pipping; "if I'm not helped off this beast I shall drop off, and if I don't have something to eat and drink I shall die."

"Landlord," said Pipping, loftily, "help down the missus—ahem! Missus Ribstone Pipping."

Vampa obeyed, and narrowly escaped being borne to the earth and flattened by his weighty lady-guest, for she literally fell into his arms and sent him staggering back.

But he was a strong old man, and, recovering himself, assisted Mrs. Pipping into the inn,

Coriolanus and his father dismounted in a stiff-legged way, after the style of inexperienced riders after a rough equestrian experience, and they walked into the inn with their knees very wide apart.

Vampa escorted them into the back room, which all three eyed with much disfavour.

" Is this the best place you've got ?" asked Ribstone Pipping.

" It is, signor," exclaimed Vampa. " We are poor, having so few English lords to serve."

" I can't sit down on these hard seats," whined Coriolanus.

" The young signor can have a cushion," said Vampa.

" Well ! yes," said Ribstone Pipping, " you may bring cushions for three. I can do with one. The saddle on the back of the mule is a collection of bumps and bits of a broken handsaw.

" You have no guide," hinted Vampa, " to look after the mules ?"

" We had one," replied Ribstone Pipping ; " but he got beastly drunk with the only bottle of wine we had—my wine, you understand--and fell off his mule. Our brutes brought us on here. We tried to stop 'em lots o' times, but they would come on, blow 'em—ahem ! dash 'em."

" I shall go off," said Mrs. Pipping, " if I don't have a little wine."

" Wine, landlord, at once !" said Pipping ; " the best. I can pay for it. We ain't travelling around without a pound in our pockets."

" All English signors are rich," muttered Vampa, as he left the room.

His first care was to get a bottle of wine and take

it to his guests. Then, having got an order for dinner and beds, he hastened to his wife in the kitchen.

"Where is Beppo?" he asked.

"He is sulking upstairs," she answered.

"Go—send him to me," said Vampa; "then get some dinner for these English people."

"What—more?"

"Yes; it is so. These are good times for Varsanta. He should be made rich for life."

"But we must be always poor."

"We have to obey Varsanta, and he tells us to watch for strangers for him. Go and send Beppo to me."

"Are these strangers young and handsome like the others?" asked Signora Vampa.

"A woman's question. *No* · get you gone, and do as I tell you."

His wife left the kitchen, muttering to herself, and Vampa stood with his back to the hearth waiting for Beppo.

In a few minutes the boy appeared, halting in the doorway and eyeing his father with a very bitter expression of face.

"Come in, my son," said Vampa, kindly.

The boy came one step into the room and halted again.

He had no faith in his father, even when he was oily.

"Why have I been locked in my room to-day?" he asked.

"Because Papita insisted on being the Englishmen's guide, and I knew you would wrangle with him," replied Vampa. "I wished to avoid that."

"**Why should Papita rob me?**" demanded Beppo.

"The Englishmen wished to have me for a guide. I could have earned money."

"Do not bandy words with me," said Vampa. "I sent Papita—enough. Now you can earn money another way. Go at once to Varsanta and tell him I have three more birds for his plucking. He will reward you for that."

"I have had nothing to eat for hours," said Beppo.

"Take some food with you and eat it on the way," said his father. "Lose no time, the hour is late."

Beppo went slowly out of the room.

Having closed the door he turned round and indulged in a series of derisive actions, expressive of his contempt for his father's commands.

"You stopped me this morning," he muttered. "I stop myself to-night. I will not go."

And now an incident occurred which shows how much may hang on little things.

It also illustrates the necessity of civility all round.

As Beppo was sauntering down the passage Coriolanus came out of the public room, and not seeing the young Italian in the dusky light, ran violently against him.

"Get out of the way, you dirty little beggar!" cried Coriolanus, aiming a blow at him.

Beppo had picked up a little of our tongue from his father, who in his early days had been valet to an Englishman. He understood by the words and the action what the other meant.

"You fault—not me," he said.

"I'll punch your head if you come near me again," said Coriolanus.

"What?" said Be

"There it is for you," said Coriolanus, striking the boy.

Beppo did not attempt to return the blow.   Nor did he say anything.

He only drew back and laughed.

"I'll take the grin out of you," hissed Coriolanus. "You miserable little brat!"

He rushed at Beppo, who vanished in double-quick time.

Coriolanus, full of the pride of victory, sauntered back to his father.

"I've just fought an Italian boy and licked him," he said.

"Good!" returned his father.   "British pluck for ever.   It's just what I used to do when a boy.   I once nearly killed a lad with a hurdy-gurdy.   He called me 'Beef,' or 'Bif,' as he put it.   I went for him at once."

"I am surprised at your allowing Cory to fight," said Mrs. Pipping.

"He's got to somehow show these foreigners that he's superior to anything foreign," replied Ribstone Pipping.   "Cory, my boy, you have done well. There's half a dollar—or it's quiverlant in the trumpery coin of this country—for you."

Yes! Coriolanus had done well, certainly.

By his arrogance he had roused Beppo to do his father's bidding, and the boy was now on the way to Varsanta's haunt to tell him that "three more birds were waiting to be plucked."

CHAPTER V.

ON the summit of a hill, shut in by a circle of mountains, stood the castle of Buenveto, a massive picturesque erection of stone.

It was only approachable by one narrow path, partly natural and partly artificial, for, save in one direction, the hill was too precipitous for any man other than an expert mountaineer to climb.

One man cannot take a castle, nor could ten or twenty, and it is safe to say that there were not many men in the district fifty miles round who would have attempted it.

For the main pass was so constructed that it had at least a score of abrupt turnings, each one of which could have been defended by a handful of men against a host, and it was commanded throughout by the battlements of the towers of the castle.

The family to whom it originally belonged died out early in the century, and for many years the place was given over to ruin and decay.

But though wind and storm injured the face of it the heart remained sound, and when Varsanta, the brigand, took possession of it he had practically an mpregnable stronghold. The only way to capture him would have been to starve him out, and that had, hitherto, not been attempted.

With a sympathetic fraternity around him it would have taken a small army to do it.

For two years or so prior to the opening of our story he had done nothing to excite public attention.

Enriched by ransom money, he had been living at ease, but his money-bags were now getting empty, and he was obliged therefore to be at his old pranks again.

We have seen how he captured Percy Winter and Will Gordon, and we must follow them to their prison room in the castle.

It was a cell on the ground floor, with one small window overlooking a precipice of about six hundred feet descent. This, to the eye from above, presented a far from inviting way out of captivity.

They were brought up to this room, their bonds removed, and then they were left to get over their injuries the best way they could.

Nothing in the way of food or drink was given them, and the following morning found them stiff and sore, weak with hunger, and parched with thirst.

But, undaunted, they stood together by the grated window, surveying the scene with the feelings of newly-caged birds.

" I wish I had listened to you, Will," said Percy. "You were right in your presentiments. I shall never laugh at them again."

" I can't say that I expected anything so bad as this," replied Will, dolefully ; " but here we are, and what we have to think of is how to get out of it."

"How is your head?"

"Hardly in thinking order. I suppose I must have a very substantial cranium, or the way they dragged me up here would have settled me."

"I surmise it is the old game—ransom," said Percy, "and I expect it will have to be paid. But I shall want time to communicate with my own banker at Naples."

"Ransom to that hound, Varsanta!" said Will, between his teeth. "The very thought cuts me to the quick."

Their conversation was interrupted by the sound of a key being thrust into the lock. The door opened, and Varsanta, with half-

stood forward, with his hand upon his hip, and affected with considerable success to be quite at his ease.

His men held their rifles ready to use if necessary.

"Gentlemen," he said, "you must pardon me for leaving you to pass the night alone. It was scant courtesy to my friends, but in my haste to drink your good health I drank too much, and so passed the night in forgetfulness."

"In other words," said Will, coolly, "you made a beast of yourself; but that was to be expected."

"Signor," said Varsanta, "you do not come from a polite nation, and I expect no soft lan-

consideration for my feelings, as I am an Italian gentleman."

"A *what?*" asked Will.

"A gentleman," repeated Varsanta. "In my veins runs some of the best blood in the country. It will be as well not to rouse me to act out of the usual course."

"And what may that be?" asked Percy.

"To treat you as guests or gentlemen until ransom is paid."

"And if it is refused?"

"In that case," said Varsanta, shrugging his shoulders, "we have peculiar methods of treating those who have ceased to be guests and become prisoners."

"You begin by torturing," said Will, "and finally kill them."

"That is, I believe, the usual method of all gentlemen in my profession," said Varsanta. "It costs some trouble to capture our prisoners, and we must get some sort of satisfaction out of them."

That the man, despite his handsome appearance, was a remorseless fiend when he chose, was perfectly clear. In as few words as possible he had made the real position of his "guests" clear to them.

"From what I learn," he went on, "one of you is the banker for the pair. One is rich, and the other is not. I believe it is you, signor?"

He turned sharply on Percy, who, by way of an answer simply smiled.

"Your answer, signor?"

"I have no answer to give a brigand!"

"I think I am right," said Varsanta, unmoved. "I shall, any way, act upon the assumption. The ransom I want is twenty thousand pounds. Your

it within a week."

"And if it is not obtained?" asked Will.

"The usual course will then be taken," replied Varsanta.

"Unfortunately for you," said Will, "you are wrong in your ideas. It is I whom you ought to retain. Let my friend go?"

"No, Will," said Percy, hurriedly. "I will not allow you to run any risk on my account. It is a rash attempt at self-sacrifice, for you know as well I do that I could not obtain such a sum without communicating with my agents at home. Your demands," to Varsanta, "are unreasonable."

"I have named the sum I want," returned Varsanta, "and when I have done that I make no abatement."

In a careless fashion he tilted his broad-brimmed hat on one side, and, taking a silver mounted case from his pocket, extracted a cigar therefrom, and proceeded to light it.

Is there such a thing as magnetic communication between two close friends?

Whether there is or not, the same idea flashed through the minds of both at the same moment.

Varsanta was engaged in lighting his cigar.

His men, relaxing a little from their vigilance, were exchanging whispers.

Why not dash at them, and make a bold run for life and liberty?

At the worst they would be as well as they were then, and, if slain, quick death would be preferable to captivity and torture.

No sooner thought of than acted upon.

Despite their weakness and the injuries both had

received, they dashed at the brigand and his men.

A good, straightforward English blow between the eyes laid the brigand chief sprawling.

Then, in an instant, the line of brigands was broken, men cast right and left, and the two friends were out of the cell. Will, with ready wit, pulled the door to after him.

One dexterous turn of the wrist and the brigand and his followers were locked in.

For an instant the two friends paused to breathe.

" Done !" gasped Will.

" And well done !" replied Percy.

The enraged brigands were now hammering at the door, and, by way of alarm, some of the men were firing shots out of the window of the cell.

In a few moments the whole of the band would be on the alert.

There was not a moment to lose.

" Do you know your way out of this confounded place ?" asked Will. " I was *non compos mentis* when they brought me in."

" I have some idea of it," replied Percy. " Follow me."

The outside passage was only dimly lighted through crevices in the wall, but they could see their way, and Percy, strengthened by the hope of liberty, hurried on to a door facing them.

Opening it they found themselves in a large hall, with a massive marble table in the centre. Chairs and forms were scattered about, and there were signs of a recent drinking bout, in which the brigands had been indulging.

From without came the cries of men calling to

door at the far end, when it was thrust open, and half-a-dozen armed men dashed in.

The door did not fall back close to the wall, and the two friends, standing quietly behind it, were hidden from view.

The brigands were exchanging hurried communications, and they had, one and all, hit upon the idea that the prisoners had made an attempt to escape.

On they went, without looking behind them, through the banquet-hall to the passage beyond, where they disappeared.

"I have made a mistake in my hurry," said Will. I left the key in the door of the cell."

There was no time to waste in vain regrets over that, and darting out of the hall they closed the door behind them.

A sweeping motion of the hand showed that there was no key there, and so they went down a short passage to yet another door, which Will opened.

A courtyard met their gaze, and beyond it was the main gate of the castle, *open*.

Outside that was a stone bridge, spanning a chasm, and then the open country.

Like greyhounds they fled across the courtyard, and reached the gate.

But from out its shadow sprang three men, who closed upon them, and in a chaotic struggle they tumbled prone upon the bridge.

Will closed with one man.

Percy had two to contend with.

A splendid wrestler was Will, and in two seconds his opponent was sent over the parapet of the bridge—down—down seventy feet below.

He struck the rocks below and lay still.

But Will, in the very act, lost his balance, and rolled over the bridge, clutching at its stone coping and making frantic efforts to hold on.

He succeeded in doing so long enough to see Percy desperately struggling with his assailants, and another brigand coming to their aid.

Then his fingers slipped and he fell.

"This is certain death," flashed through his brain, and in the tenth of a second he summoned up before him all the friends he knew, and wished them adieu.

CHAPTER VI.

PAPITA AGAIN ACTS AS GUIDE WITH COMPLETE SUCCESS—VARSANTA SEES UNTOLD WEALTH AHEAD.

R. RIBSTONE PIPPING was heard to observe—

"I don't exactly see how the opposite direction can be a short cut back."

"Signor, it is so here."

This was the answer of Papita, who was professedly guiding the Pipping family on their way back, their own guide not having put in an appearance.

One night at the inn had been enough for them, and as the difficulty of again riding the mules, keenly felt by father and son, was got over by having some sacking laid on the saddles and sitting sideways, Pipping *père* saw no reason for remaining longer.

His spouse would rather have rested another day ; but she hardly counted in a family discussion, and, although "ready to drop" every moment, she allowed herself to be assisted into the saddle to make one of the party.

Papita, as we have recorded, was again guide, and he led them away to the mountains, a "short cut," as he vowed, by all sorts of saints, human and inhuman.

"Of course, a short cut is desirable," said Ribstone Pipping, shifting a little in his saddle, "for really—dash it—I don't find sitting sideways much relief. How are you getting on, Cory, my boy ?"

"How do you think I am likely to get on ?" whimpered Coriolanus. "Ain't I half-flayed ?"

"Don't worry the boy," said Mrs. Pipping. "He must be suffering dreadful."

"Allow me to state, Mrs. Pipping," said her husband, with strained politeness, "that at the present moment *I* don't look upon mule riding as a luxury."

After this they rode on with a silence unbroken, save by an occasional gasp or stifled groan from father and son.

Papita, holding the rein of Mrs. Pipping's mule, led the way, and the others followed.

In two hours they were well among the hills, and halted for a rest.

After the painful process of dismounting, Ribstone Pipping walked up and down to "stretch his legs."

The stretching process, we may remark, was confined to gently sliding one leg before the other, with an occasional sudden stop to ease off a little pain.

Some refreshment was partaken of—mainly in a liquid form—and then they went on again.

"It seems to me," said Ribstone Pipping, "that we are going over the hills and far away. I hope, my good man, that you are not making a mistake."

"No mistake," said Papita. "We first go up to ze count's castle—go in a minute, zen on—home."

"The count's castle!" exclaimed Pipping. "What count?"

"Ze Count Varsanta," replied Papita, gravely. "He hear of you, and say bring ze Englese gentleman—let me see him."

"It's very civil of him," said Ribstone Pipping, "and I don't mind looking in on the count; but don't lose your way, for I can't stand much more of this saddle business. Oh! dear. It's like being rasped with a file."

It was a longer ride than Pipping expected, but he was consoled by the prospect of visiting a count. Indeed, they were all flattered by it.

What a fine thing it would be to talk about when they got home.

"What did you say his name was?" Pipping asked. "Magenta?"

"Varsanta, signor, replied Papita. "Ze oldest family—best count in Italy."

"Perhaps if he were to know how I'm suffering," said Pipping, "he would let us stop for the night."

"He is sure to ask you," replied Papita, with a quiet grin.

pointed out to them they were all quite overcome with its grandeur.

"So massive," said Pipping; "the house of a monarch."

"It isn't far short of Windsor," remarked Mrs. Pipping.

"Don't you talk about Windsor," returned her husband. "Windsor isn't within miles of its grandeur. What do you say, Cory?"

The boy, out of pure opposition, replied—

"It looks more like Woking prison than anything else."

"A prison!" laughed Pipping. "That IS a good joke."

"Most excellent," said Papita, and then they all laughed together.

The toilsome way up to the castle was borne bravely, and the sure-footed mules carried them without mishap.

As they crossed the bridge over the chasm, Pipping shuddered, Coriolanus turned white, and Mrs. Pipping shut her eyes.

With a parapet so low it was very trying to the nerves.

They were evidently expected.

At the gateway two of the "count's" retainers received them with a rough imitation of an English military salute, to which Pipping responded like a monarch acknowledging a subject's greeting.

Mrs Pipping smiled, but Coriolanus went wrong again, by surlily declaring that "they looked like organ-grinders."

"Really, Cory," said Ribstone Pippin, as his mule stopped and he hastily descended to the

are ungracious—with such a hospitable reception, too."

Several "retainers" had now come forward to take charge of the mules, and a keen observer would have noticed that they were all struggling to repress some emotion very like mirth.

Papita, doffing his hat, bowed low, and bade the guests follow him.

"Now, Jane," said Pipping, "carry yourself as if you'd got some go in you. Don't wobble. Hold your head up. We are here to represent the proudest empire on earth."

"I can't help rolling a little," said Mrs. Pipping. "I ain't use to counts, and I don't mind telling you, Ribby, that I'm ready to drop."

"If you drop," tartly replied Pipping, "you won't find me stooping to pick you up. I wouldn't do it. Steady, here we are."

Papita, having ushered them into the first passage, leading to the great hall, opened a door on the left, and threw it open with a flourish.

"Enter," he said. "I will inform the count of your arrival."

It was a fair-sized apartment they were ushered into, well-furnished, with an eye to comfort.

Two couches, half-a-dozen chairs, an ottoman, a handsome inlaid table, some specimens of armour, and a quantity of rich marble looked very effective.

There was also a guitar lying in a chair—an evidence of the musical taste of the "count."

"Ribby," said Mrs. Pipping.

"Well? What?" tartly asked her husband.

"I feel I can't stand it. I'm going," she gasped.

"Cory," said Pipping, hurriedly, "take your

mother out into the yard and leave her there. We can't have no fainting nonsense before counts."

"I think you might take her yourself," replied the amiable boy. "I want to see the count as well as you do."

The appearance of Varsanta cut short all questions about retiring for any of them.

He came into the room with a quiet, cat-like step, holding his head erect, as a nobleman ought to do.

He was attired in a suit of red velvet, trimmed with lace, rather a faded get up, but impressive in its way.

"Welcome," he said, "to my humble home."

"Humble, do you call it?" exclaimed Pipping, as they shook hands. "I call it a slap bang up crib —place—ahem! *abode*. My wife—Mrs. Pipping —Jane, drop that gasping; it isn't society manners —my son, Coriolanus, known as Cory for short."

The pseudo Count Varsanta shook hands with all, assisted Mrs. Pipping to a chair, and pushed forward two others for father and son.

He took one himself, and entered on an agreeable conversation about the weather.

"I find it somewhat lonely here," he said, after awhile, in excellent English, "and I trust you will make a stay with me."

"We don't mind putting up for the night," mpressively replied Pipping; "but a long stay wouldn't suit us."

"A short stay, then," said Varsanta, serenely. "And now, with your leave, I will take your lady wife to the countess."

"Certainly," said Ribstone Pipping, "I've no objection to that. Now, Jane," in a whisper to his wife, " pull yourself together.   Put a bit of cheek on, and don't let 'em fancy you ain't used to society."

Mrs. Pipping answered with a faint smile, and rose up.   Varsanta offered her a hand and led her to the door.

" Now that's manners," exclaimed Ribstone Pipping, admiringly.   " I see you know how to go it, count."

The expression of Varsanta's face was that of malvolent delight, but Pipping did not observe it. The brigand and his lady guest disappeared.

He was absent about a quarter of an hour, and when he returned he presented a somewhat ruffled appearance—there was also a slight scratch on the tip of his nose.

The cause of these marks of disorder will be apparent anon.

" Now, signor," said Varsanta, " allow me to show you to your room."

As they passed down the passage, Ribstone Pipping paused here and there to point out what he considered ought to be done to the place.   He wished the " count " to understand that he was quite at his ease.

" You don't seem to go in much for wall-papers here," he said.   " A neat thing of blue-ground and gold stars would improve this place immensely. The ceiling ought to be whitewashed also."

" Ah !" said Varsanta ; " these things cost money. You are rich, perhaps."

Ribstone Pipping looked at him and smiled.

" I've made a pound or two," he said.   " My cheque is good for a biggish amount."

think I could about empty one of your blessed banks if I tried."

"Signor," said Varsanta, grasping his hand, "you make me rejoice. I am glad."

Pipping was a little astonished at this demonstration, but he soon understood what it meant.

Varsanta turned aside just before he came to the banquet-hall, and ushered his guests down a narrow passage—very dark.

At the bottom was a door, which he unbolted and threw open.

"This is your room, my rich friend," he said.

Ribstone Pipping found himself in a chamber that was about as inviting as the condemned cell in Newgate.

The walls were bare, and the principal thing in the way of furniture was a rough table. The only seat was a stone slab let into the wall.

And last, but not least, the window was a heavily-barred, glassless aperture, about a foot square.

"Well, this is a rum crib," exclaimed Pipping ; "ain't it, Cory ?"

"A beastly coal-cellar !" said Coriolanus.

"It is your resting place, signor," said Varsanta, politely.

"Eh ?"

"Your chamber."

"Come, none of your larks," said Ribstone Pipping. "Surely you've got a better place than this ?"

"Yes," said Varsanta ; "but this is *your*

countess have got over their confab we will get along."

"Stand back !" cried Varsanta, drawing a glittering stiletto, " or you are a dead man."

" I—I—don't understand you," gasped Pipping.

" A few words will make all clear," replied the other. " I am Varsanta the brigand, and you will be my guest until I receive a ransom in proportion to your riches. Anon I will let you know the sum I require."

He slipped back, closed the door, locked it, and father and son were left together to make the best they could of a very bad business.

" Cory," gasped Pipping, " am I dreaming ?"

" How should I know," sobbed Coriolanus. " Oh ! what a horrible mess you've got us into."

" Me, my boy," said Pipping. " I don't see that I'm to blame in the matter. It's Varsanta the brigand is it ! We heard some stories about him when we were at Naples."

" And you said it was all fudge," moaned Coriolanus.

" Did I ?"

" Yes, and you said also that if you ever came across him that you would let him know what it was to tackle a Britisher. You didn't try to tackle him. You were scared out of your wits."

" I was took aback," said Pipping ; " but after all nothing much may come of it. I daresay a tenner will satisfy him."

" You've got more than that about you."

" So I have, Cory ; but I'll put the rest in my boots. Short Wellingtons are handy for that sort of thing. Help me off with them. And, mind this, Cory, that you don't say a word about what I'm going

hundred pounds in my pocket. Why on earth did I have so much about me?"

"Because you are so fond of showing your money and bragging," said Coriolanus, as he knelt down to pull off his father's short Wellingtons, Pipping being seated on the stone slab, "and you've told him you're rich, too. I've read about brigands, and I know that he won't let you off for a thousand. Oh—oh! and he won't let me off at all."

"It IS a gashly business," groaned Pipping, "and there's your poor mother, too. It will kill her. She's down in asterisks by this time. A count! The lying thief. Pull away smart, Cory. I hear somebody coming."

CHAPTER VII.

NOT DEAD YET—BEPPO TO THE FORE.

T was Varsanta, who had come to honour Ribstone Pipping with another visit. He entered the cell with two armed brigands behind him.

"Friend Piping—" he began.

"Excuse me," said Ribstone, "Pipping—Pipping."

"Piping or Pipping, what matters?" said the brigand. "You are rich—it is enough for me. I have settled on your ransoms—twenty thousand pounds for yourself and ten thousand each for your wife and son."

"How much?" gasped Pipping.

"Forty thousand in all," said Varsanta, easily. "Not a stiver less."

He motioned to the brigands to retire, followed

them out, and the door closed upon the wretched prisoners.

"You heard that, Cory?" said Pipping.

"I aint deaf," answered Coriolanus, surlily.

"Forty—thousand pounds!"

"It all comes of your bragging about being so rich."

"My son," said Pipping, "harrow not a father's feelings at this awful time. I feel as if my head was going off. Let us lie down and try to sleep."

. . . .

From out a strange turmoil of ugly dreams Will came back to life.

He looked around and found he was lying on the edge of a jutting piece of rock, while over his head were, the

some of them broken.

Then the recent past flashed across his mind up to the time of his fall. He saw how his life had been mercifully spared. But what of Percy?

Had he escaped? Will hoped so, and it seemed probable.

Then he examined himself, to see if he had any broken bones, and, finding none, peered over the rock to the depths of the gulch below.

The bottom was quite fifty feet down, but there were small facilities which a man of activity and possessed of a cool head could avail himself of, and without any mishap he reached the bottom.

There, to his surprise and no

came suddenly upon two persons—one living and the other dead

The first named was the brigand, who had been left to lie there and rot by his fellows, and the second was the boy Beppo.

Doffing his hat, the boy said—

"Your servant, signor."

"Beppo," returned Will, "I was your friend yesterday, and I want you to help me now."

"Signor, I would die for you," replied the boy.

"Better live for me," said Will, with a smile.

He then questioned Beppo about his friend, and, to his great sorrow, learnt that Percy had been dragged back into the castle.

"And they have placed him in the west cell," said Beppo, "for I heard Varsanta give the order."

He explained to Will that this cell was only accessible from the outside by means of a precipitous cliff, "hard for those who look down to climb," said the boy.

"But it can be climbed?" said Will.

"Yes, signor."

"And you know exactly where that cell is?"

"Oh! yes, signor; I have been all over the castle, in and out. I know it as well as I know this," holding up his hand.

Will, always full of resource in a time of difficulty, immediately conceived a plan which might possibly be successful.

"Beppo," he said, "you would help my friend if you could, I am sure?"

"Signor," answered Beppo, "as I would die for you—so I would for him."

"Good—I believe you," said Will. "Now you must do three things for me—get me a stout iron bar, show me the way up the cliff, and point out where I can find the cell. Is there an iron door to it?"

"Not on the outside, signor. I will go with you. I will do all you ask."

First of all it was necessary to get out of the gulch and find a hiding-place for a few hours. Beppo said he knew of a hundred.

"And you are safe, signor," he said. "They will not look for you near the castle. They think you have run away—far off. They are in pursuit."

This was welcome news, for it would give Will a chance of working without interruption.

By some means they had failed to see him fall over the bridge, which probably arose from Percy's gallant struggle for liberty occupying their whole attention.

Beppo led the way round the gulch to a spot where they could ascend unseen, and from thence by a somewhat devious route he escorted Will to a clump of trees growing at the base of the almost perpendicular cliff.

This was the west side of the castle, and that was the cliff which would have to be scaled.

Will saw that it would require some skill and a great deal of coolness to accomplish it, but he felt that he could and would do it.

Beppo assured him that he would be safe in the wood, "if he did not show himself outside like a rabbit," and sped away on his quest for a crowbar.

He did not say where he was going, and he was many hours away.

At last, late in the afternoon, he returned to the anxious Will with a crowbar and some bread and fruit.

"I have been to the house of a friend of mine named De Lustra for these," he said.   "He was not at home, so I took them."

"It is enough for me that they are here," replied Will.

The food was welcome, simple as it was, and having partaken of it, Will declared himself ready.

By the direction of Beppo he fixed the crowbar in his attire, so as to leave both hands free.

"You will want them, signor," said the boy.

CHAPTER VIII.

WELL DONE, WILL—VERY ROUGH ON RIBSTONE PIPPING—SOMETHING LIKE A WIFE.

P—up, like two flies crawling on the wall, went the boy and man, with the glory of the setting sun shining upon them, until their scaling task was almost accomplished.

The summit was at hand when the sun went down, and in the brief twilight they performed the rest of their dangerous work, and landed safely on level ground.

After a short rest, much needed by both, Will looked to the right and left, and saw that he was standing on a narrow platform of rock about four feet wide, running along the greater part of that side of the castle.

Beppo, after a glance at the wall, located the position of the cell by touching two places not fifteen feet apart.

"It begins here and ends there, signor," he said.

Then Will brought out the short crowbar and went to work.

.   .   .   .   .   .

In a dark cell, without so much as starlight to relieve the gloom, Percy paced to and fro, disconso- and brooding over the fate of his friend.

What had become of him he did not know, but he feared the worst.

"Perhaps he is dead," he thought; "if so, I should like his spirit to come to me, even though the sight of it should carry out the theory of Cole-ridge and kill me."

Tap—tap—tap!

A sound on the outer wall.

Percy sprang to it, and with his foot gave three answering sounds.

Tap—tap—tap!

"It *is* Will," he gasped. "Oh! faithful friend. Though what can you do for me but share my fate? I wish you, for the first time, a hundred miles away."

It was the wish of pure unselfishness, the wish of a true friend.

Percy could not quite understand what was going on, but he knew that an effort was being made to release him.

Every now and then would come the "Tap—tap —tap," and it seemed to him that each one was appreciably nearer than the last.

But the hours passed, and his friend did not come.

"Perhaps it's some fiendish piece of mockery," he thought—"a jest of those ruffian brigands."

As he thought this the door opened and Papita swaggered in.

The door was immediately closed again and locked.

"Signor," he said, with a flourish of his arms, "behold in me the ambassador of the great Varsanta."

"I behold in you," replied Percy, "a contemptible and most loathsome scoundrel—nothing more."

Papita laughed, and, crossing the cell, leant against the outer wall with folded arms.

"You are angry, signor," he said, "because I cannot always play the humble servant. But I am too bold and great to be for ever servile. I am Varsanta's right hand."

"Well," said Will, "what do you want?"

"An order for your ransom to be paid, or you—"

He said no more, for suddenly the wall behind him yielded.

There was a noise of iron rattling against stone, and then Papita fell with a huge mass of stone upon him.

It was done in a moment, and he was pinned to the floor of the cell as securely as if a stake had been driven through him ten feet into the earth.

Upon Percy there fell a flood of light, pouring through the opening, and against the golden background of the morning sky he saw the outline of a well-known form.

"Will!" he cried.

"Quick! lose not a minute," was the answer.

Give me your hand. That's it—free again ! But. steady—look not down."

"You may trust my nerve," said Percy. " I am braced up for *anything* by the sight of you."

.   .   .   .   .   .

There were sounds of alarm and strange cries in the castle—a rattling of doors, a stamping of feet, and Ribstone Pipping was awakened from a beautiful dream, wherein he was the guest of the Lord Mayor.

Starting up, he fell off the stone bench on which he had passed the night, and uttered a yelp of alarm.

This awoke Coriolanus, who opened his eyes, stared about him a moment, and then uttered a howl.

" Oh ! I'd forgotten all about the brigands," he cried.

" So had I, my son," replied Pipping; " but—alas —alas ! we are here."

" I wish they'd bring me some breakfast !" moaned Coriolanus.

" Perhaps they will," said Pipping, soothingly ; " I hear somebody coming."

Immediately afterwards four brigands entered the cell.

Two were armed, a third carried some iron fetters of the good old Newgate pattern, and the fourth had a hammer and some rivets.

Without any preliminary nonsense they proceeded to garnish the forms of Pipping and his son with these ornaments.

Both were temporarily deprived of the power of

expostulation, but as the job of fixing the fetters was about finishing, Pipping asked—

"What's all this about?"

"You Englese dogs escape much," replied one of the men, "so ve make you sure."

Then they left their prisoners to digest their position, and make the best of it in their power.

The footsteps died away, and a silence, somewhat weird, fell upon the castle.

Not a sound was heard save the clanking of those awful fetters as the wretched wearers shifted uneasily to and fro.

Half an hour passed—a time of dismal anxiety.

And then footsteps were heard again, also the voice of a gentle woman.

The voice of Mrs. Pipping.

"You get along," she was saying, "or I'll blow your head bang off."

"Goodness gracious!" exclaimed Pipping. "What new horror is coming to us?"

"Unlock the door," cried Mrs. Pipping.

The door was unlocked, and Luiji the brigand appeared. Behind him was Mrs. Pipping, armed with a musket.

"Go in," she said, "and you two come out."

Luiji, with a gesture of despair, obeyed, and father and son came wonderingly forth.

"Lock the villain in," said Mrs. Pipping, "and bring away the key. He was on guard over me, and he told me all the rest were out after some runaways, so I up and at him, and I got his gun, and I made

"You didn't," she said ; "but you thought your-self a wonderful man.   But you are *not*   Go ahead. That's the way out."

The road to liberty was clear. All the other brigands were gone in pursuit of Percy and Will, we may assume. Even the outer gate was unlocked.

Across the bridge, and down the narrow pass outside, went the Pipping family, the jangling of fetters being a sort of musical accompaniment to their movements, and soon they put half-a-mile between them and the castle.

"My dear," said Ribstone Pipping then, "permit me to express—"

"Silence !" answered Mrs. Pipping, who was marching with the gun upon her shoulder. "I can hear people handy. It's them brigands. In mercy hide somewhere or you are a dead man !"

CHAPTER IX.

SYLVIO DE LUSTRA AND HIS DAUGHTER—BEPPO'S GOOD WORK—THE ADVANCE OF THE BRIGANDS.

OT more than a mile from the brigands' castle, on the far side of the village, stood a peasant's homestead, surrounded by a few acres of grassland.

It was hemmed in by the huge hills around it, and formed a veritable oasis in a mass of rugged land.

This quiet home among the mountains was occupied by one Sylvio de Lustra and his daughter, Aura.

They were of a good family, but had been brought down in the world, how we may presently show, and as unfortunate people in our great cities hide away in the courts and alleys, so did Sylvio de Lustra select a home where he was little likely to be troubled by his fellows.

On the morning when Percy and Will made their attempt to escape from the brigands, father and daughter were standing at the door of their house, looking curiously in the direction of the castle.

The turrets of the huge building were visible above the top of an adjacent hill, and on the hill

fro.

"Something is wrong, Aura," said Sylvio de Lustra. "Those rascals are busy searching for somebody who has escaped them."

"I pray they may not fall into the villain's clutches," said Aura, clasping her hands.

She was a typical daughter of sunny Italy—slim, dark-eyed, olive-skinned—fair as woman is in that beautiful clime when Nature is not interfered with by the arts of the toilet.

A lovely creature, surely, and at the age when her beauty was just in full bloom.

"Oh! how I hate the dogs," said De Lustra, between his teeth. "Had we a better government they would not be in existence another day."

They stood there watching until the specks disappeared, and then they went into the house.

Although small it was well furnished with things that had once belonged to a nobler building, and in the nick-nacks, the pictures, and the general embellishment of the place there was evidence of a refined taste.

Over the hearth several rifles of modern make were suspended. Sylvio de Lustra took them down one by one and examined them.

"All loaded," he said. "It is well to make sure, my child. We may want them."

"But, surely, they would never dare to attack us?" said Aura.

"Varsanta has of late become somewhat imperious," replied the Italian, thoughtfully. "He urges his love in spite of all the rebuffs we have given him. It is possible that he may attempt to seize us both by a *coup de main.*"

"Father," urged Aura, "let us leave this place, where at any time we may fall victims to Varsanta's malice."

"My child," said her father, bowing his head, "I love my country, and I am too poor now to live save in seclusion. Would you go to Naples to herd with the *lazzaroni?*"

"No—no!" exclaimed Aura, with a shudder

"This place is *mine*," pursued De Lustra; "all I have left to call my own. I cannot sell it, for who would buy? No, here we must remain—at least, for awhile. Perchance Varsanta may be slain, and then we shall have no cause to fear."

"I pray for his death," said Aura, "although I fear it is wicked to do so."

"Without him his band is nothing," continued her father. "They would fly to pieces like a bundle of sticks suddenly loosened."

"Father!" exclaimed Aura, "a footstep."

The old man hurriedly took down one of the rifles, and, bidding Aura bar the door, rushed to the window.

Looking out, he saw a boy walking towards the house. Lowering his gun, he said—

"It is only Beppo, Vampa's son. Admit him."

Aura, who had barred the door, drew back the bolts and Beppo came into the room.

Doffing his cap, he bowed low, first to Aura, and then to her father.

"What brings you here, Beppo?" asked De Lustra.

"Signor," said the boy, "you have a kind heart."

"Aye—aye, boy! That is the usual opening to a petition."

men—Englishmen—who are flying from Varsanta They have escaped from the castle."

" Beppo," said Sylvio de Lustra, " I know you as a companion of these brigands. Play no tricks upon me."

" Signor," replied the boy, " these Englishmen saved me from my father when he was angry. He beats me bitterly in his wrath. I owe these English signors a debt. I wish to pay it."

" If they are watched and seen to enter here," said De Lustra, " Varsanta will lay siege to the place. I am fully occupied in defending myself. I hardly dare run the risk, for my daughter's sake."

" Father," said Aura, earnestly, " we must not think of that. Go—bring them here, Beppo. They shall have such shelter as we can give them."

The boy looked at De Lustra, who waved his hand and simply said—

" Go."

Beppo breathed a blessing on their heads and darted away.

De Lustra looked gravely at his daughter.

" It is a terrible risk," he said.

" You are thinking of me," she answered; " but I care not for Varsanta Do not fear. If the worst comes I shall not fall into his hands. The grave is open to one bold enough to strike."

She touched her girdle significantly, and her father understood her.

Concealed in a pocket, made for the purpose, was a small, keen stiletto.

It was terrible to think of the possibility of using it on herself; but that would be better than falling

the Englishmen approaching. Beppo was skilfully
guiding them along a line of fruit bushes, so as to
conceal them from the view of anyone looking from
the direction of the castle.

In a few moments Will and Percy were within the
house.

Greetings were exchanged, and our friends
expressed their gratitude for the shelter offered
them.

"It is nothing," said De Lustra, simply; "you are
welcome."

Percy was a little lame, and, sitting down, rubbed
the ankle of his left foot with his hand.

"I slipped a few feet when descending the cliff,"
he explained to Aura, who looked at him sympa-
thetically.

"I have an ointment," she replied, "which will
speedily cure it."

She was engaged in putting some bread and fruit
upon the table. De Lustra passed into an inner room
and brought them a bottle of wine.

"It is not of the best," he said, "for we are poor.
But such as it is you are welcome to."

They thanked him again, and, with Beppo,
partook of the simple fare.

All were hungry, having fasted many hours.

As they ate they told the story of their escape to
their attentive host and hostess.

The descent of the cliff, Will declared, "had been
a succession of miracles," and but for being in a
highly strung condition, arising from joyous excitement, they never would have accomplished it.

As it was, they had slipped more than once, and
been saved by some projecting stone or the roots of
shrubs growing in the crevices.

Percy fell fifteen feet at the finish and sprained his ankle, but not seriously, as he declared.

Aura listened, shuddering more than once. To her and De Lustra it was almost incredible that such a feat had been accomplished.

Beppo came in for his share of the adventure. He simply answered—

"I did it for the kind English signors who saved me a beating."

During the narration De Lustra went several times to the window and looked out to see if any of the brigands were approaching.

For some time he saw nothing to occasion alarm ; but presently he beheld several brigands, like blood-hounds on the trail of a slave, advancing and closely scanning the ground.

"Signors," he said, "our foes are coming. It is for you to say what is to be done."

"We will not bring trouble on your house," replied Percy, readily. "For ourselves, we would like to fight these fellows if we had the weapons."

"There are weapons," said De Lustra, with a sweep of his hand towards the rifles, "and I have a hundred cartridges ready for use."

"No," said Will, resolutely. "To attempt a defence would be to run the risk of bringing death, or worse, upon your charming daughter. The first shot would bring the whole band down upon you like a pack of wolves. We will leave you. Have you a back way out here ?"

"Yes," said De Lustra ; "but you shall not use it. I have one part of the house which will serve you to hide in. I see it is repugnant to your feelings, and contrary to your natural courage ; but you are considerate."

"We should be ungrateful brutes," said Percy, warmly, "if we did not do anything for your daughter's sake."

"Come, then," said De Lustra, "the boy can remain here. They know him and will see nothing suspicious in his presence. Aura, remove all signs of the food. I will return to you immediately. Signors, two rifles and some cartridges are at your service."

He opened a box standing on a small table against the wall, and took from it a handful of car-

tridges, which he divided between them.

Then with a glance through the window as he left the room he assured himself that he had still a few minutes to devote to his guests.

Percy and Will each bestowed a glance of mingled gratitude and admiration on Aura, and then followed him.

Beppo and Aura hastily cleared the table, removing all signs of the recent humble feast, and then the latter once more barred the doors.

E LUSTRA led the way through a room that was a contrast to the one just left. The furniture was very poor, and there were signs of its being rarely used.

On one side was an open window, close to which was an old deal table and a chair or two.

On the right, opposite the window, was a door, which their host opened, disclosing a cellar about three feet below the other part of the house.

It contained an old wine-press, long disused, a few boxes, some bottles, and a varied collection of discarded rubbish.

Behind the press was another door, which opened with a sliding action.

When closed it had the appearance of being nailed up.

"It is a large cupboard," said De Lustra, "and there is a bolt inside by which you can secure the door. It will seem to them to be fast if they should enter here."

He drew aside the panel, and they passed into a huge, dark cupboard, far from inviting; but it was as good a place of concealment as they could hope for.

De Lustra closed the door, and gathering up some dust from the floor, rubbed it into the crevice where it opened. It then looked as if it had not been opened for years.

Having heard the bolt shot he was satisfied, and returned to the front room just in time to hear a knocking at the door.

He hesitated for a moment, and then opened it. Confronting him was Varsanta, accompanied by half-a-dozen of his band.

"You keep your house close, neighbour," he said.

"It is my custom to keep the bolt fastened," replied De Lustra.

"Ah! who have we here?" said Varsanta, peering into the room. "Beppo—the one I am seeking —may I have a word with him?"

He did not wait for permission, but entered, and, after doffing his hat to Aura, addressed Beppo.

"Boy," he said, "how long have you been here?"

"An hour, great Varsanta, perhaps a little more," replied Beppo.

"Have you been near the castle this morning?

Beppo nodded.

The boy was wonderfully cool, having braced himself for an ordeal.

Sylvio de Lustra leant against the mantelpiece and looked at the ceiling.

Aura brought out some needlework and sat down behind the brigand.

Neither dare look at Beppo, for fear the brigand should detect some passing sign of intelligence.

"Saw you anyone—any strangers?" asked Varsanta.

"Yes, two Englishmen," replied Beppo.

"Save us all," thought Aura, "he is about to betray us."

Her heart almost stood still with fear. The hue of her father's face became ashen.

Varsanta, however, had his back to both, and could not see their signs of inward trouble.

"And whither were they going, these Englishmen?" asked Varsanta.

"They were skulking through the dry watercourse," said Beppo—"in this direction, I think. I have no more to tell you of them."

It was an evasive reply, but it apparently satisfied Varsanta, who smiled and drew a cigar from his vest pocket.

"Sweet Aura," he said, "may I crave a light?"

There were a few sticks quietly smouldering on the hearth, and Aura, rising, walked to the fire and stooped to raise one of the burning brands.

In a moment Varsanta had thrown his arms about her, and held her fast.

At the same instant her father was pinioned behind by the other brigands.

Both were helpless prisoners.

Whether it was a concerted plot or not, it was, from Varsanta's point of view, well done, and he laughed in a quiet way.

"Now don't struggle and ruffle your charming plumage, my pretty bird," he said, banteringly. "Better yield to the most gentle snarer that ever spread a net."

"You are a coward and a villain!" said Aura.

"So—so, perhaps," answered the brigand; "but hard words fall like feathers upon those who do not

On De Lustra a dumb despair had fallen.

It was useless to cry out or struggle, for in a trice his arms had been secured, and Aura was helpless in the hands of her captors.

And, again, both thought of the guests, who would assuredly, on hearing any outcry, come out to the rescue. Why should they be sacrificed?

It was a noble instance of self-abnegation.

By the direction of Varsanta a scarf was put through Aura's arms and fastened behind, so as to have her secure without hurting her.

"You see how gentle I am," he said. "You scarcely feel your bonds?"

She did not answer him.

"And now, boy," began the brigand, "I— Why —gone?"

Yes—Beppo had vanished, and although they looked for him outside the house they could see no signs of him.

"It does not matter," said Varsanta; "he is scared and has run home."

Other members of his band now appeared, and he ordered his captives to be taken outside.

CHAPTER XI.

BREAKING OUT.

SINGLING out four of his men, Varsanta coolly gave them the following instructions —"Pack up everything valuable which you can carry, and bring them on to the castle. Then fire the house—it will not be wanted any more. Henceforth Signor de Lustra and his

"I beseech you not to fire the house!" cried Aura, wildly.

"Why not?" asked Varsanta. "It is so poor a place."

She was thinking of the two young men in hiding, who were threatened with a horrible death; but, although half distracted, she had the wit to say—

"It is my home—spare it!"

"For your sake I will," replied the brigand, in a low tone, "although it is not my custom to recall a command. And I will not plunder the place, but simply have your possessions carried to rooms appointed for you in the castle."

He signed to the men who had charge of the captives, whispered a few words to the rest, and, having lighted his cigar with a match he drew from his pocket, gaily sauntered off.

With his head down, the poor signor, surprised and defeated, followed next, and then came Aura, walking firmly enough, her eyes flashing.

She felt at ease, for had she not that little stiletto in her belt?

That, as a last resource, would open the way to freedom—the freedom of the grave.

The four men left in charge of the cottage were in no hurry to begin their work.

Their first idea was to see if there was anything to drink about the place.

Having found the remnant of the bottle of wire brought out for Will and Percy, they finished it, then they wandered into the back room, and from thence into the cellar.

While rummaging there they talked and laughed loudly, and the muffled sound of their voices reached the ears of the men in hiding.

Percy, who had the bolt in his hand, pushed back the door a quarter of an inch to listen.

The brigands having failed to find more wine, for the hospitable signor had brought out his last bottle for his guests, were leaving the cellar, jesting over the capture of Aura.

It was enough for Percy.

Half-a-dozen whispered words to Will and the door was pushed back.

Out they went, as they hoped, to the rescue.

The four brigands heard them coming. One made for the door, another essayed to leap out of the window, a third got under the table, and the fourth stood his ground because fear would not allow him to run away.

"Stand !" cried Percy, in Italian, as he entered the room, followed by Will, "or you are dead men."

The man at the window leapt for his life, and Percy fired.

Instead of alighting on his feet the brigand turned half over and pitched upon his head.

He had been shot like some carrion bird upon the wing.

The man who had made for the door escaped, but the other two remained.

They had weapons, but seemingly had lost all power of using them.

"Come out of your shelter !" said Percy, kicking the fellow who was under the table.

He howled like a well-whipped cur.

Just as Percy was about to drag him out, Beppo, in a breathless state, appeared in the doorway.

"Signors," he said, "hasten away. Varsanta with a dozen men is returning hither."

CHAPTER XII.

THE PIPPING FAMILY GO THROUGH A COURSE OF TRIBULATION—BACK AGAIN.

AS we left Ribstone Pipping and his family at a critical moment of their lives, we must now, in common justice to these hapless people, return to them.

It will be remembered that an alarm had been given, and the fear of the coming of the brigands took possession of them. Flight was impossible.

The buxomness of Mrs. Pipping was against her, and Ribstone Pipping and Coriolanus were too heavily fettered to make a run of it.

In despair they cast their eyes around.

"Here's a hollow," said Mrs. Pipping, hurriedly; "I think if we—"

"Get into it quick," interrupted her husband.

The hollow she referred to was a hole under the shadow of a rock, about two feet high and as many wide. If there was room for all three inside, it would make a capital hiding-place.

"Get into it, I say," repeated Ribstone Pipping; "Jane, you first."

"Just like mother," whined Coriolanus; "she doesn't mind what becomes of *me*."

"Oh! you ass. There, go on," said his father, and Coriolanus, nothing loth, did so.

Mrs. Pipping followed, and managed, with a little assistance, to get through the opening.

"It's all right, Ribby," she said—"lots of room."

Pipping crawled in, accompanied by the music of his clanking chains, and he was none too soon. Barely had he settled down when two Italians—a young man and an old one—came up the path, looking curiously about them.

"What sounds were those we heard, Alberto?" said the old man.

"It was a tinkling of bells, Gorka."

Gorka shook his head sadly and wisely.

"No bells," he said. "It was more like the music made by my wife with her iron pots and pans when something has raised her wrath."

"It is strange," rejoined Alberto, "and I see no cause for it. Dost think that it was evil spirits? I have not been to mass lately."

"It may be Satan himself, for all I know," said Gorka; "but I do not fear it."

"Ah! thou art brave," sighed Alberto. "While I am weak and foolish. Shall we rest?"

"Right willingly."

They sat down sideways to the hollow where the Pippings were in hiding, suffering tortures because they were afraid to move or speak."

The two men entered into a conversation which the listeners did not understand, and it is of no moment to the reader, being merely a discussion about the merits of certain sheep and goats.

The two men were shepherds, who had come to the hills in search of some of their flock, which had disappeared.

If only straying they would be found ; but if stolen by the brigands—why, there was an end of them.

"For goodness sake don't move the twentieth part of an inch," whispered Ribstone Pipping. "Cory, what are you rubbing your nose for ?"

"It itches," replied the amiable boy, in a tone rather louder than was necessary.

One of the men outside pricked up his ears.

"By the saints," he said, "I hear another strange sound."

"What is it ?" asked his comrade.

"A hissing—like that of a serpent."

"Then it must be in that hole."

They both stood up, and each taking a stone in his hand, they waited for the serpent to issue forth.

Perhaps they were bold enough to stand their ground because no such a thing as a serpent had ever been seen in that country.

"It is nothing," said Gorka, after rather a long silence.

He was preparing to sit down again when he received a shock which made him leap fully a foot in the air, and then alight in a sitting position.

The cause of it was as follows—

Ribstone Pipping, thinking of his son's nose itching, immediately found his own getting uneasy.

He rubbed it, but that only made it worse, and within his nostrils the elements of a sneeze began to gather.

Compelled to remain still, he made a great effort to keep back the much-to-be-dreaded explosion.

But it was of no use.

"At-t-t-i-chew !"

It was an awful sneeze, and the hollow cave,

although of limited dimensions, had a big echo in it.

It also caused Pipping to throw up his arms, so that there was much rattling of chains.

"Santa Maria!" cried Alberto; "it is a fiend. Away, Gorka! Run for thy life!"

But Gorka could not get up, much less run. All he could do was to sit there and feverishly breathe fragments of prayers for his safety.

Alberto, however, ran down the hill, leaving his aged comrade to his fate.

He sat there, staring hard into the opening, and soon made out two fiery optics fixed upon him.

They were the harmless eyes fixed in the harmless head of Ribstone Pipping.

"It *is* Satan!" gasped the old man, and then he felt that it was all over with him.

Ribstone Pipping, noting the fixed gaze of the old man, fancied they were discovered, and, in a fit of desperation, determined to come out and beg for mercy.

Accordingly, he essayed to issue forth, but no sooner had he put his head outside than Gorka gave it a most unmerciful whack with a stick he carried.

"Oh! murder," shrieked Pipping, and his voice, in the hollow of the cavern, sounded like the roar of some huge beast.

Poor Gorka! He could not run, but he could roll, and, falling on his back, he commenced his retreat by turning over and over.

He was seen to disappear by those inside, and the cause of his rotatory motion being guessed at by Ribstone Pipping, he suddenly became very brave.

"There is nothing to be afraid of," he said. "We may safely go out again."

"Oh! it's awful," sobbed Coriolanus; "it's a shame! It will kill me, and then you will both be sorry."

Ribstone Pipping muttered something under his breath and crawled out. Coriolanus followed, and Mrs. Pipping then essayed to do the same.

But for some reason she could not wholly succeed. Half-way out she stuck fast.

"It's my improver, I think," she gasped.

"Go back and take it off," said Pipping

But here again arose a difficulty—she could not move either way.

"Why don't you pull me out?" she gasped. "I never saw two such noodles in my life!"

"Try!" said Pipping, desperately. "Lay hold of the other arm, Cory! Now, then, both together!"

But the more they tugged the more fixed she seemed to be, until, to their utter amazement and terror, a terrific explosion took place, and Mrs. Pipping, released, came out with a run.

"It was that rifle!" she gasped. "I forgot it, and it was fixed across the hole somehow. Ribby, I think I am wounded somewhere. I am dying!"

"Oh! don't say that," cried Pipping, pathetically. "It isn't the time or place."

"Anyway," said Mrs. Pipping, "I don't walk about in public. My dress behind is all blown to pieces."

Such, indeed, was the case.

Of the improver of the hapless lady's dress nothing now remained but a tangled mass of wire, on which fluttered a few bits of rag.

A portion of her dress as big as a drumhead had also been blown away, exposing to the human eye a

"You go on, both of you," she wailed. "I'll stop here and die."

"Don't talk in that way," said Pipping, soothingly. "I assure you it isn't so bad as you think."

"Never again," said Mrs. Pipping, slowly rising, "will I be lured to these 'ere foriegn lands by you. It's all your purseproud rubbish, Ribby, that brought us here. You wanted the Frenchies to see how flush you were of cash. Go along and leave me to die."

Ribstone Pipping winked at Coriolanus to move on, and, as he expected, his wife quickly altered her mind. She was soon after them, bitterly reviling the author of her misery.

Fortunately for them, they were perfectly safe from the brigands, who were scouring the country in the opposite direction, and they eventually succeeded in retracing their steps to the open land. It was a long and weary march, and they suffered much.

Had it been suggested the day before that they could have performed the journey under the circumstances, they would have declared it to have been impossible.

And, furthermore, fortune favoured them by meeting a peasant with a mule and cart, who was bearing towards the village.

He was so petrified by their appearance, that at first he could do nothing but stand still and stare at them. But Ribstone Pipping made him understand by signs that he desired to be taken to the village, and that he would pay him well for the job.

The man agreed to take them, and they were

by signs, for they could not understand each other's language.

It was a most unsavoury vehicle, having at no distant date been used for agricultural purposes of the lower order.

What could be worse in the way of conveyances? But it was better than nothing, and they were silently thankful.

It was close upon sunset when they were brought up to the door of the inn, where the staggered Vampa was talking to two or three of his village acquaintances.

" Here we are," said Ribstone Pipping, affecting a jollity he did not exactly feel. " Have you got a blacksmith in this place, to take off these—*ornaments ?*"

" Signor," exclaimed Vampa, in English, " ze meaning of zis, I beg ?"

" It means brigands—thieves," replied Pipping, "and murderers ; but we've done 'em—me and the missus between us—and saved our brass. They haven't got a penny out of us."

Vampa, completely in the dark about the events of the day, assisted his guests out. Mrs. Pipping, too tired to think of the ruined improver, was first led into the inn. Pipping and Coriolanus followed, the former withhis bragging cap on.

" Yes," he said, " we've done 'em. No brigand can come it over a true-born Britisher. That 'ere Varsanta won't forget our meeting, I'll bet. My missus had better go upstairs at once and tidy herself a bit. Me and Cory will wait here for the blacksmith."

Vampa ran into the kitchen to his wife, and hurriedly told her what had happened.

"What is to be done?" he asked.

"The irons must come off," she said. "The gendarme comes his round to-night."

"But what will Varsanta say?"

"Fool! are not these people as safe in our clutches without irons as with?"

"True," replied Vampa.

There was not a blacksmith in the village; but Vampa knew how to remove the irons, which he speedily did with a hammer and chisel.

A small crowd of marvelling men watched the operation, which took place in the public room.

As for Ribstone Pipping, he stood erect, with folded arms, in his own estimation the hero of the hour.

"Yes," he said; "we did him. I should have thought it odd if a brigand got over *me*."

"Signor," said Vampa, quietly, "will you tell me all about it?"

"After dinner," replied Pipping. "We ain't had anything to eat. Oh! give that fellow with the cart a little loose cash, and put it down in the bill."

"You say, signor, the brigands did not take your money from you?"

"Not a stiver—bar a few of your miserable bits of silver and copper. I've saved the bulk on it. I've got the pile about me. Hurry up with something to eat, and let me have a bottle of wine at once."

They went into the room they had previously occupied, and before they got far with their wine Mrs. Pipping joined them.

She had made herself presentable by sacrificing the ruined improver and stitching up the hole in her dress.

. . .

"Give me some wine, Ribby," she said. "I'm ready to drop."

He gave her half a tumblerful, and she revived a little, butshe was not any-thing like herself until dinner was ready. They all ate well, and Ribstone well. Pipping drank as well. He became boastful, and talked of the way *he* had brought them safe out of the brigand's haunt.

"I'm the wrong sort of man to be crowed over by that lot," he said. "Whenever you are in trouble, Jane, you can rely on *me*."

Coriolanus was fast asleep on the settee and had nothing to say to his father's version of the day's pro-ceedings. "By - the - way,"

wine, "I may as well put them bank-notes back into my pocket."

He pulled off his short Wellington boots, and brought out from the first he dived his hand into an indistin-guishable mass of paper. The other contained nothing better. Ribstone Pipping, in his wan-derings that day, had trodden the notes into pulp. He stared at the ruined notes, then at his wife, then at the sleeping Corio-lanus, and then gasped out—

"Oh! here's a go. We are alone in a far off country, without a blessed penny to keep our-selves with."

"But your banker at Naples will help you," she said.

"My banker!"

I've only got an order on him—and that's been trodden up with the rest.   It's ruin, old gal—ruin !"

———

CHAPTER XIII.

A RUNNING FIGHT — CUNNING VERSUS COOLNESS.

PERCY and Will, who were, as the reader knows, suddenly warned by the boy, Beppo, did not exactly relish the information he brought.

It was clear to them that the firing of the gun had given the brigands tidings of their presence in the house, and Percy reproached himself for having in his haste used so noisy a weapon as a rifle.

But they wasted no time in vain regrets, and, having bestowed another hearty kick on each of the remaining brigands, they asked Beppo if there was a back way out of the house.

"There is, signors," replied the boy. " I will show it to you."

The brigands who had been so heartily kicked lay grovelling on the ground, and, Beppo, as he led the two friends from the room, was favoured with baneful glances, that boded ill for him in the future.

The boy saw them, and perfectly understood his position.

Henceforth his life would not be safe in his old haunts. But what cared he?

Had he not said that he would die for the kind signors, and what he said he meant.

From them he had received kindness and protection, such as he had never known before, and the secret spring in his heart had been touched, letting out the better nature of the boy.

Behind the house of De Lustra was a small farm yard, but there were no cattle, only half a dozen goats.

Beyond it, for a quarter of a mile, there was open country, and then the hills again.

"I do not see how we can get away without being seen," said Will. "Let us stay here and fight it out."

"We might carry on a running fight," suggested Percy; "but, of course, if you wish to stay, I will remain."

"My dear fellow, I am with you. Beppo, my boy, you run on ahead. It strikes me that you will get into serious trouble if the brigands lay hold of you."

"A fig for them!" said Beppo, snapping his fingers. "I can hide for weeks, months, and they will not find me."

"Away, then," said Percy. "If we are captured do you think you can get to Naples?"

"I *would* do it, signor."

"Well, then, if it comes to that, go to the British Ambassador and give him this card. Tell him what has happened to us. If he cannot send us help in time he may be able to avenge us."

Beppo took a card Percy drew from his pocket, and sped away towards the hills.

The two friends proceeded more leisurely in the same direction.

"It won't do to run," said Will, coolly; "we are sure to want all our breath for fighting."

If they had any doubts on that score they were speedily dispelled by the appearance of Varsanta, with eight or nine men at his heels, the majority armed with rifles.

They poured out of the back door, yelling like infuriated wild beasts, but came to a sudden stop when they saw Percy and Will slowly backing, with their rifles ready for use.

"It is useless to spare the brutes," said Will. "Pick out a man, Percy, and drop him. We will fire one at a time."

Percy saw that it would be madness to indulge in any qualms as to the use of his rifle, and, rapidly sighting one the foremost men, he fired.

Possessed of a good eye and being a practised sportsman, he sent the bullet home.

The brigand aimed at leaped into the air and then fell upon his face with his arms spread out.

The others yelled, and those who had rifles fired back, but with a very wild aim.

No harm was done to the two gallant young fellows.

"Are you ready?" asked Will.

"Loaded," replied Percy.

And then Will fired, and a second brigand was seen to fall.

The rest spread out, seeking any place that afforded them cover Varsanta showing more cool-

Walking leisurely towards the wall of the farm-house, he stopped for a moment to light a cigar with the end of one he had been smoking.

Percy covered him with his rifle.

" Shall I bring him down, Will ?" he asked.

" The fellow has pluck," replied Will ; " but so has the tiger and the panther."

" Then here goes," said Percy, as he pulled the trigger.

But at the same instant Varsanta moved forward again, and the leaden missile missed him by a inch or two.

He must have heard the scream of it as it rushed by, for he involuntarily skipped a pace, and then resumed his nonchalant manner.

" No," said Will, " he is not sound.   He is only a blackguard bravo after all."

Varsanta by that time had gained the corner of the wall, and, being the last to seek refuge, they had now all disappeared.

The two friends continued their leisurely retreat, looking behind them every few seconds, but for a time saw nothing.

At length, when they were a good five hundred yards from the farmyard, they saw the brigands breaking away to the right and left, extending themselves into an open line.

But they were still careful to keep well out of the range of ordinary rifle-shot.

When the line was fully extended the two ends began to advance, until the brigands formed a semi-circle round our friends.

To add to the peril of the position other brigands were coming up, each in his turn making for one or

At first Percy and Will thought they intended to make a ring round them; but that was not their idea.

Steadily they advanced, forcing the friends in the direction of the hills, where it was plain they hoped to take them at a disadvantage.

The probabilities were that they would be able to do so, for they knew the country, and Percy and Will were strangers to it.

It will be readily seen that the brigands might easily get into a position to have these young men at their mercy.

The only hope for the retreating friends was in the possibility of their keeping them at bay until the night had come on.

Under cover of the darkness they might escape.

Percy ventilated his idea, and Will saw in it the one chance of escape.

"Then go easy," said Percy—"crawl. Not one of these fellows will dare to come nearer, so long as we are in open country. Our two friends are night and Beppo."

"That is not so bad for you," replied his friend; "but both at present are some distance away."

"The night will be here in two hours."

Ping!

One of the brigands on the left had tried his luck at a pot shot at them, and the bullet went whistling by.

"This must be put a stop to," said Will.

Turning towards the man who had fired, he took steady aim at him, and it was almost ridiculous to see the fellow dodging to and fro to avoid the dreaded pellet of lead.

...... up, each in his turn making for one or
the other ...... of the attacking ......
OR, BRAVERY ......

Will followed his movements with the rifle, but did not fire until the brigand, scared out of his wits, wheeled round and began to run.

Then Will fired.

All eyes were on the retreating man, and when he was seen to fall a yell burst from every brigand's throat. But they made no attempt to close in.

Acting on their ideas of prudence, they stood still for awhile, and allowed the two friends to get further away.

Then when, as far as firing was concerned, they were pretty safe, they advanced again.

"On my word," said Percy, "I believe if we dashed at them they would all run."

"But they might not," said Will. "Our safety lies in the hills. The sun is getting into the west. Go slowly."

We need not follow them through the manœuvres of the next hour or so. They were simply a repetition of what had been done before, save that the brigands fired no more.

They came on like men bent on entrapping some wary animal of the chase.

Apparently they made no effort to drive their quarry in any particular direction; but nevertheless Will and Percy were insensibly pressed towards a ravine, which was like a chine cut in the hills.

At a glance it seemed to offer them every chance of safety, for it looked like a place that could be defended with ease.

It was a pass that half-a-dozen men could hold against an army, provided, of course, that the army kept upon level ground.

But, on the other hand, it had an element of danger which escaped the two friends.

Once in it they could not emerge therefrom if a single man were there to guard it.

And although they did not know it, that pass was blind.

It was simply a rift in a hill—a huge crack that only went half way through.

There was no outlet on the other side, and the cliffs were too precipitous to scale.

Of course this was known to the brigands, to whom every inch of the country was familiar, and with secret exultation they saw the gallant fellows voluntarily advance to the trap.

But they gave out no sign of their delight.

No warning note of triumph was uttered to stop Will and Percy, who reckoned that they had reached a haven of safety.

"Once there," said the former, "we can hold it until the night comes, and then we can go on."

The pass was reached at last, and they paused at the mouth of it to deliberately scan the semi-circle of foes.

The weapons on both sides were at rest.

With the butts of their rifles on the ground, the parties arrayed in minor warfare surveyed each other.

From the west came the slanting rays of the setting sun, throwing long shadows across the ground, and gilding the hills with a scarlet hue.

Afar off, bathed in a misty radiance, the huge castle inhabited by Varsanta frowned upon the fair land around.

No sound broke the stillness save the faint, far-off bleating of the goats that had strayed from De

Nothing, in a quiet way, could be more impressive than the scene, and the two friends were deeply moved by it.

"There goes the sun," said Percy; "it seems to be setting rapidly."

"I feel as if some dear friend were going away from me—for ever," replied Will.

"Peace, man of presentiments," said Percy, with a laugh that was somewhat forced.

"I cannot help what I feel," said Will. "No man can still the movements of the soul. Here"—touching his breast—"lies something that is me, and yet beyond me. It speaks to me in certain times and seasons, and although all it has told me has not quite come true, it has never wholly lied."

"Well, Will, we must take things as they come."

"I must do so, but not you, Percy. I am only a poor, penniless artist, of no particular good to myself or to others. The world will not miss me. But with you it is different. You are rich. Your family has high hopes of your future, and you are simply travelling to fit yourself, by a knowledge of men, for a great career."

"Never mind that old fellow."

"But I must mind it, for it was in yielding to a fad of mine, to go out of the beaten tourists' track, that has placed your life in peril."

"Look here, old man," said Percy, "if you give me any more of your self-reproaches I swear to you that I will make a rush at those fellows, and end the whole business as far as I am concerned. Hang it all, I came freely."

"Then there is an end of it, and, look, down goes the sun. Let us each scare these fellows by taking a couple of pot shots at them. You try your hand at that fellow with the red sash, and I will devote myself to Varsanta."

CHAPTER XIV.

IN THE TRAP—CAPTURED—A RUN FOR LIBERTY —AGAIN AT THE CASTLE.

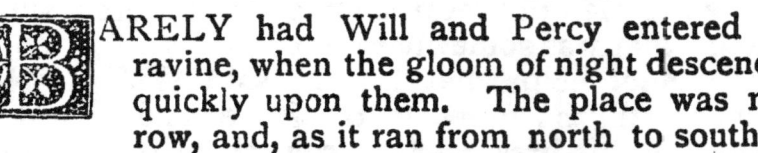ARELY had Will and Percy entered the ravine, when the gloom of night descended quickly upon them. The place was narrow, and, as it ran from north to south, at once caught the shadows of the coming darkness, and to Percy it was even chilly.

"What a ghost-haunted hole it is !" he said. " Look at the rocks. They might be hobgoblins."

" It is a fantastic place," said Will, quietly, "and the sooner we are out of it the better."

A few minutes later they found they were not likely to get out of the place in a hurry.

Suddenly it rapidly narrowed until it was impassable, and they saw the end of it.

It was almost dark now, but their eyes, grown accustomed to the gloom, enabled them to make out that they were in a trap.

Then the object of the brigands' movements was clear to them both.

" Done !" said Percy, with a stifled groan. " There is nothing more left for us but to go back and fight our way out."

"Nature did a scurvy trick when she fashioned this place," said Will ; " but let us return. Perhaps we may make a successful rush of it."

Having examined their weapons, and found them ready for use, they began to retrace their steps.

Notwithstanding their efforts to go quietly, they stumbled here and there, for it was very dark, and minor obstacles were not easily seen.

Overhead there was a dark blue sky, spangled with stars.

Not a sound, save that which they made in walking, broke the quietude of night. Not a whisper—not a movement—betrayed the presence of the brigands.

The young adventurers reckoned they would find them at the mouth of the ravine, but when they arrived within easy distance of it none of the villains were in sight. Percy and Will halted, and held a short whispered conference on the position.

That some form of ambush was prepared for them they could not doubt.

It was hardly possible that the brigands, after having driven their quarry into a snare, would give them a chance of escape.

"Let us go on," said Will, after an exchange of surmises, "and keep our eyes about us. As soon as we are attacked, fire once and then use the clubbed rifle."

"Just so," said Percy, laconically.

But in one respect they were no match for the brigands, and that was in low cunning.

They expected to find the ambush just outside the ravine, whereas the band were in hiding just within it.

Naturally enough, the two friends stopped at the mouth of the place to look about them.

That was the brigands' opportunity.

A dozen ruffians leaped up from behind fragments

of rock that were lying about, and sprang upon the young men.

Taking them in the rear, they had them at a disadvantage.

The rifles could not be fired save to waste the powder and shot, nor could a good, honest blow be dealt to any of the assailants. All Percy and Will could do was to struggle for freedom.

And even in that respect they could do little, for they had been seized garotter fashion round the neck, and, their heads being bent back, they were almost helpless.

Well, impossibilities cannot be done, even by the most heroic, and they were soon secured by the exultant brigands.

"Harm them not," cried Varsanta. "Let us respect the geese that are to lay the golden eggs."

His mocking tones exasperated Will, who quickly answered.

"You will get no golden eggs from me you scurvy scoundrel."

"Ah ! we shall see," said Varsanta, walking up to him, and snapping his finger in Will's face. "It is the old song ; but Varsanta never was foiled yet. It would take birds with stronger wings than you have to fly away from him."

The arms of the prisoners by this time were securely bound, and the brigand chief, having examined the knots and approved of them, gave the word to march forward.

"Walk easy," he said, with a sneer. "Let us be considerate to our English friends, who must have had a very fatiguing day."

At this the other brigands laughed, and Percy ground his teeth.

It was hard—very hard to bear. So much toil, and to end in this.

But neither he nor Will answered the brigand.

Nor did they take the slightest notice of the taunts which he continued to pour upon them as they marched along.

They were mostly of the bantering form, mock congratulations on their daring, and sneering regrets that all their labour had not ended more auspiciously.

At last Varsanta began to get exasperated.

"What ! Will you not answer me ?" he cried. Shall I slap your face, and make you speak ?"

Again no answer.

In a fury he stepped up to Percy, and gave him an open-handed smack on the face.

We all know what strength fury will sometimes give us.

It gave Percy a strength he had rarely, if ever, known before.

The deadly insult of the blow roused all that was passionate in his nature, and with one great effort he burst his bonds.

The crack of them was like the snapping of a carter's whip.

The sound was followed by a shout of joy from Will, and a yell of alarm from the brigands.

"Run, Percy," said the former ; "better for us both Run !"

Percy saw in a moment that it would be madness to remain, and abandoning his first impulse to endeavour then and there to rescue his friend, he struck out right and left and darted away.

Two brigands were bowled over by the blows he dealt, and although neither were seriously hurt.

they rolled about the ground uttering cries of pain.

Verily a clean hit between the eyes is hard to bear by those who are not used to fisticuffs.

Will, of course, had made an effort to get away also ; but a dozen hands held him fast.

Some shots were fired in the direction Percy had taken ; but no immediate pursuit was attempted.

All that Varsanta did was to despatch a couple of scouts to give warning to some of his band, who were parading the public roads towards Naples.

Will no longer despaired.

He became quite jaunty as they moved on again, and even chaffed Varsanta on his loss.

"The only goose that could lay a golden egg is gone," he said. "You have my entire sympathy, especially as it appears that you are now so poor."

"A curse on you Englishmen !" hissed Varsanta. "You are not men, but serpents—eels ! There is no holding you."

Will Gordon laughed heartily—the wrath of the brigand amused him. Presently Varsanta said, quietly enough—

"You have a proverb at home that he laughs best who laughs last—our little play is not yet over."

"No," said Will, gaily ; "but it is shorn of some of its interest. The chief character has dis-appeared."

Now, although Will was in this humorous mood, he knew that Varsanta need not utterly despair.

Getting clear away from the neighbourhood could not be accomplished without some successful manœuvring.

And, again—would Percy beat a retreat without making a grand effort to help his friend ?

Assuredly not, although Will heartily wished he would.

Well, at any rate, he was free for the present, and that was a matter for congratulation.

By-and-bye, if ill fortune worked in favour of the brigand again, it would be time to grieve.

With a light step he kept up with the brigands, and, beyond an occasional jocular remark, said nothing to them.

The castle was reached, and Will saw that it was better guarded than before.

Two armed men were pacing up and down the bridge, the gates were closed, and when opened by the command of Varsanta disclosed other guards within.

"Throw that dog into one of the lowest dungeons," said Varsanta, "where he will have some company. He has been very merry on the way hither. Let him be merry now he is here—if he can."

man in utter loneliness will cling to *anything* for companionship.

After all Varsanta was not far wrong.

They were companions, those toads and lizards, and what not, of the dungeon.

" I would exchange a million of money for a good meal," he muttered ; and then a curious buzzing was heard in the cell.

He looked around him to see from whence it came, and could find nothing to account for it.

It was all fancy.

This was the herald of coming delirium, and well he knew it, having some knowledge of such things.

He did not dread it, but rather hailed it as a coming relief.

" Delirium and unconsciousness are akin," he said. " I shall at least know nothing of it."

And then he lay still, patiently awaiting the coming mental darkness.

At that hour Varsanta, seated in one of the more airy chambers of the castle, was partaking of breakfast.

This cut-throat, this cold-blooded ruffian, was partaking of all sorts of luxuries peculiar to the country.

Though all his band starved he must be well fed, for he was the chief.

There were wine and fruit, and preserves, biscuits, and some toasted larks on toast, with many other things to tempt the palled appetite.

And very little appetite had the brigand.

His eyes were heavy, and his cheeks flushed, evidence of excess over night.

But there was more than an ordinary debauch to account for the dark cloud upon his brow.

He was drinking, but eating little. A bunch of ripe grapes lay on a plate untasted, untouched. His mind was busy with other matters.

Suddenly he struck a handbell upon the table, and Luiji appeared.

"Have you seen Papita this morning?" he asked.

"Yes, chief."

"How is he?"

"No better. He has no use in his limbs, and the doctor says he will never walk again."

"Then there is an end to him," said Varsanta, brutally. "He will only be a burden and a hindrance to us. Let him be disposed of."

"Great chief, how?" asked Luiji, whitening under the tawny hue of his skin.

"You ask me that!" cried Varsanta, angrily. "Is there nothing you can do without being directed like a child?"

"The choice of death has always been in your hands, great chief," said Luiji.

"It is so," said Varsanta, grimly. "Then let him be dropped down the old well. It is dry and will never serve us again. How deep is it?"

"There were two hundred feet of rope in the windlass when it was there," answered Luiji.

"A grave deep enough for an emperor. Send him down," said Varsanta. "Now as to the lady you have charge of. How fares she?"

"As proud and defiant as ever."

"Ah! well—so let it be. I like a proud woman. Beware, however, lest she overcome and befool you as the fat old woman did. Or, stay, it can be prevented. Set her free."

"Chief!"

" You hear me.   Give her the run of the castle. She cannot get away—every avenue is closely guarded—but keep her father close.   They must not communicate with each other."

Luiji went away, and an hour later presented himself again before his chief.

Varsanta, meanwhile, had been heavily drinking.

" Well, what now ?" he asked, savagely.

" Papita, chief."

" Yes, of him—what !"

" He is gone."

" Ah ! and how did the dog take his fate ?"

" He cursed you and all of us. Begged for mercy. Asked to be laid out in the air, to die by inches. His yells of terror as we hung him over the well were piteous."

" No doubt," said Varsanta, curtly ; " he was the sort of man to yell when his own toes were trodden on.   Is that all ?"

" No, chief ; there is no tidings of the escaped Englishman."

" But there will be soon ; he is in hiding. Anything more ?"

" The other Englishman cries out in his cell."

" Good ! I have taken the courage out of him."

" Chief," said Luiji, " he has gone mad ; he is raving."

" A madman," said Varsanta, " is of no use to himself or his friends."   Here he poured himself out a bumper of wine.   " Let him follow Papita."

Luiji stared at his chief aghast, and ventured to remonstrate.

" A dead dog brings no ransom," he said.

none.   Am I to give my orders twice ?   Go—release the gentle Aura, and then dispose of this raving Englishman.   We must have no madmen here."

Luiji left the presence of his chief in a troubled frame of mind.   Neither of the tasks set him were exactly congenial.

With the shrieks of his old comrade—and very awful shrieks they had been—still ringing in his ears, he had little taste for repeating the ghastly procedure.

But Varsanta had said it was to be so, and it had to be done.

To disobey the orders of their chief was to court death.

Then, again, there was Aura.

Luiji had no taste for women, and his experience of Mrs. Pipping had taught him how dangerous they could be.

That Aura had a resolute spirit he knew—and what mischief might she not work if set free ?

But it had to be done, for it was Varsanta's orders.

Aura was confined in a chamber in a part of the castle called the Round Tower.

It commanded a view of the country adjacent, and as an apartment there was nothing in it to object to.

The furniture was old-fashioned but good, and it had evidently been used by a lady of rank at some time in the days gone by.

But a gaudy cage is not appreciated by the recently captured bird, and Aura was restless and unhappy.

Towards those deputed by Varsanta to wait upon

The brigand chief, up to the time we write of, had not come near her since her captivity.

Luiji, with a foreboding heart, went up to her chamber and unbolted the door.

Then he knocked, and after a short delay Aura appeared.

"Signorina," said Luiji, backing as he would have done from a released panther, "you are free to roam about the castle."

Then he would have cleared out, but she shortly and sharply called upon him to stop.

"My father," she said ; "where is he?"

"Signorina, he is well cared for."

"I ask you where he is?"

"Signorina, Varsanta, our chief, has forbidden us to tell you."

And then Luiji fairly ran away, leaving Aura alone.

Her first step when left to herself was to see that the small weapon she carried in her sash was ready for immediate use if required ; and then she sauntered down the gloomy stairs to the chamber below.

Her release came as a surprise, and she fancied that it was preliminary to some act of treachery on the part of the brigand chief.

Therefore was she prepared to do a desperate deed the moment the need of it became apparent.

"Death, rather," she muttered, "than be the victim of that monster."

The chamber below was empty. There was not even a particle of furniture in it. So was the one below it, and then by a door she reached the battlements of the castle.

There she came upon an armed pacing brigand

to and fro. The man saluted and respectfully drew aside to let her pass.

There was something more kindly in his eye than she had seen in any of his fellows, and it led her to question him.

"Can you tell me where I can find my father?"

"Signorina," said the man, "I dare not tell you; it is forbidden."

"Tell me," said Aura; "I will not betray you, and one day I may be able to reward you handsomely."

"I ask for no reward, signorina; but I will tell you all I know," replied the man. "He is in one of the lower dungeons on the other side of the castle—I know not which."

"One thing more," said Aura; "how can I find him?"

"Ah! it is a puzzle—a maze," replied the man, shaking his head.

"Never mind that," said Aura; "tell me how to get to it."

The brigand looked carefully round to see if he was observed. Nobody was in sight.

"See yon square terrace," he said; "enter by the door, and pass to the left. There you will find another door; open it, and a winding staircase will lead you to a narrow passage that runs under the courtyard, at the end of all the dungeons. They are many—you may not find what you seek."

"I will try," said Aura. "Let me look at you, so that I may know your face again. One day I may be able to befriend you."

"Signorina, I ask nothing, I say. The saints bless your pretty face and keep you from all harm."

She looked at him keenly, and he read the meaning of her glance.

"No, lady, I cannot help you more. I am only one of many—and my life is in their hands."

"I will not ask for more," she said. "*Adios*."

To the square tower she went, and from there descended down the winding stairway to the passage he had named.

It was so dark that if she would traverse it she would have to feel her way.

For a moment she hesitated.

Might it not be that the kindness of this man was assumed, and he had sent her into a snare?

But the thought was instantly dismissed.

Shuddering, she groped her way, lightly touching the slimy walls with her finger.

After what seemed a long journey she came to a closed door.

Groping about it she found a handle, turned it, and the door opened.

Beyond was a passage dimly lighted by fissures in the ceiling, and on either side were the cell doors.

From inside one of the cells, half-way down, came the moaning of one in pain.

Could it be her father in suffering?

With a palpitating heart she ran forward, but stopped suddenly on hearing some men inside.

"It is the chief's orders and must be done," said one.

"But it is terrible," said another, "and so profitless. The chief has been drinking. To-morrow he may grow sober, and ask us why we have done this thing."

"Ah ! he will forget and call us fools."

"Down with him !" cried the other speaker, ferociously ; "the man is mad.   Of what good is he living ?"

Aura staggered to the cell speechless with terror. Was it her father they were assigning to some horrible fate.

Pushing open the door, she looked in and saw a scene which, though it relieved her as far as her father was concerned, half-stupefied her with horror.

Standing by the side of an open well, whose mouth was black as pitch, were two brigands with a burden between them, which they were about to cast down into the fearful depths below.

That burden was Will Gordon with his arms bound, and moaning and groaning in a delirious state.

She recognised him as one of the young Englishmen to whom she had, two days before, given shelter, and with a wild shriek of terror sprang into the cell.

CHAPTER XVI.

RIBSTONE PIPPING GETS DEEPER INTO THE MIRE —MRS. PIPPING AGAIN AROUSED—THE CARABINEERS.

BRIEF stepping-back must now be undertaken to see how things had gone with Ribstone Pipping and his family.

Penniless and half distracted, he went to bed after swearing in his wife and son not to say a word about their impecunious state.

"I must have a little time to reflect," he said. "Possibly I may find some means of getting out of this pass. I am considered to be a man of resource."

"By whom?" asked Coriolanus.

"Oh! you get to bed," said Pipping; "the idea of asking such a question! Boys ain't boys nowadays."

Pipping went to bed and had a restless night.

Though he was a man of resource, he did not see his way out of the fix at all. Morning came, and he arose with a heart of lead.

"You keep up your pecker," he said to his wife; "I'll see you out of this."

"You are vulgar, Ribby," she replied; "respectable people don't talk about peckers."

Pipping declined to argue the question with her, and they went down to breakfast. Vampa was there, talking to Coriolanus.

On seeing the pair, the landlord turned to them and said—

"I hope you have passed a good night."

"Middling," replied Pipping; "but, at a pinch, I could do with fewer fleas."

"Fleas in my house !" exclaimed Vampa. "It is impossible. Who ever heard of such a thing ?"

"I've not not only heard of but seen 'em," said Pipping, "but never mind 'em. Let's have breakfast."

"Signor, it shall be procured," said Vampa; and bowing, he left the room.

"There is nothing like a little bounce when you are in a fix," said Ribstone Pipping.

"We shall see where your bounce comes in when he brings the bill," replied Mrs. Pipping.

"You'll cut it then," said Coriolanus.

"Corry, I feel ashamed of you," said Pipping. "Don't forget I am your father."

"I ain't likely to," replied Coriolanus, "seeing that you tell me of it about every ten minutes."

Ribstone Pipping scowled but said no more. He was hungry and wanted his breakfast, and not in a condition to argue.

The breakfast was soon served. It consisted mainly of bread, butter, and eggs. Pipping, still keeping on the bounce, did nothing but grumble at it.

"It shall be better to-morrow," said Vampa, "if the signor will condescend to stay."

"We are here for a week," said Pipping.

"That's the way to blind him," he muttered, as

the door closed on his host, "and our game now is to go for a walk and BOLT."

It was a good plan—a most excellent plan—but for certain reasons it did not quite work.

When Pipping told Vampa they were going out, the Italian asked whither they were going.

"Oh! just for a stroll," replied Pipping. "Anywhere."

"Signor, you have escaped once from brigands. You may be again taken."

"I'm not afeard—I mean afraid of that. I'll go the other way."

"It's no safer, signor," said Vampa; "I will accompany you."

The face of Pipping lengthened out, and he was about to demur when Mrs. Pipping struck in—

"Certainly, Ribby dear, it will be for the best. We ought to have someone. Let Mister Vampa come?"

Ribstone Pipping yielded, although with an ill grace. He felt that it was all over with the bolting for that morning, at least.

Mrs. Pipping, pleading a slight lameness, borrowed a stout stick of Vampa with which she walked through the village.

Coriolanus kept by her side, Vampa and Pipping bringing up the rear.

It was not a cheerful party by any means. Vampa never was at any time a very sociable man, and Pipping was disappointed on finding his little plan upset.

Coriolanus was in his usual sulky condition, and Mrs. Pipping was grimly silent.

They took the road by which they had come to

the village, and when they had traversed a mile or so Vampa suggested they should return.

"Not yet," said Mrs. Pipping.

"The signora *must* return," replied Vampa, firmly.

"Indeed?" said Mrs. Pipping. "Who says so?"

"I do," said Vampa. "I cannot permit you for to go."

"It's my belief," said Mrs. Pipping, "that you are connected with that thievish lot of brigands." (Vampa changed colour.) "Ah! I see by your face you are."

"The signora is mistaken," said Vampa.

"Mistaken or not, we are going on."

"It shall not be so."

"Who'll stop me?"

"I will," said Vampa, whipping out a knife from his sash.

Coriolanus and his father started back, but Mrs. Pipping calmly smiled.

"I am not going to be dictated to by you," she said.

And then, before Vampa could dream of her intention, she raised the heavy stick which she carried, and brought it down upon the Italian's pate with a terrific thwack.

He went down as if a thunderbolt had fallen upon him. His knife fell from his hand.

Blinking, he lay helpless upon the ground, while Mrs. Pipping calmly gave directions to her husband to make him secure.

"Stuff a handkerchief in his mouth," she said, "and tie his hands and legs. Then let us get along as fast as we can."

Pipping, the man of resource, trembled so that he could do nothing, so Mrs. Pipping did the binding and stuffing of Vampa, and then, with a bold air, resumed the march.

"Mother !" cried Coriolanus, "there is somebody coming."

"There is always somebody coming," moaned Pipping ; " is it more brigands ?"

"No—soldiers," replied Coriolanus ; "there they are, all on horseback, coming this way—over the hill."

———————

CHAPTER XVII.

THE CARABINEERS — RIBSTON PIPPING IS APPOINTED TO A POST OF HONOUR.

THERE were about forty soldiers in all, Italian carabineers, commanded by a dark-eyed, fierce-looking officer, with a tremendous pair of moustaches.

He it was who first espied the Pipping family, with their captive, the exasperated Vampa.

Giving the word of command in an authoritative tone that could have been heard half-a-mile off, he galloped up, followed by his men, who formed a circle round the group.

"Signor," he said, in fair English, "haf I not see some leetle of you in Naples ?"

"I have been there," replied Pipping ; " indeed, we were there a few days ago."

"And how is it zat I behold you now ?" asked the officer.

Pipping, in brief, told his story, without, however, giving his wife all the credit she deserved.

It was "We did so-and-so " right through.   If

Mrs. Pipping had not been there it would have been a case of " I," without a doubt.

Against Vampa he could not, of course, make any specific charge, beyond his attempt to force them back again.

That, however, was enough for the officer.

" Dog !" he said, addressing the innkeeper, " you are in league with Varsanta. Speak !"

As Vampa could not speak while he was gagged, the " stuffing " was removed from his mouth, and then he proceeded with great volubility to protest his innocence.

" But why insist on the people going back?" asked the officer.

" It is not safe for them to go about alone," replied Vampa. " Is not the country infested by Varsanta's men ?"

" Bah !" was all the officer said to this.

They had been speaking in Italian, which Pipping did not understand ; but the officer translated it to him, and asked him what he thought of the answer.

" He is in league with the brigands," said Pipping.

Now, here we must admit that Pipping did not fully believe his assertion. He said what he did because he saw that if Vampa was kept in custody for a time he would *be unable to send in his bill.*

Thus he, by chance, in his selfish intention, hit the nail on the head without exactly knowing it.

" Get up !" said the officer to Vampa ; " fall in there. Fair lady, my horse is strong, and you are somewhat faint—will you ride behind me ?"

Mrs. Pipping had collapsed again, and was really in a semi-breathless condition. She appreciated the honour of the offer from such a handsome man, and sweetly smiled.

"I shall be glad, sir," she said, "if anyone will hoist me up."

The officer twirled his moustache, and signalled to two of his men, who dismounted, and in a trice they lifted Mrs. Pipping up behind the officer.

"Put those divine arms of yours around me," said the officer, gallantly. "Thus—now hold tightly. We will walk to ze village and deposit you."

"Where shall I get up?" asked Pipping, who did not exactly like the officer's tenderness to his wife.

"Ze gentlemans walk," was the reply.

And this the "gentlemans" had to do.

Pipping was glad of the protection of the soldiers, but he was horribly jealous of his buxom wife, who, although half scared out of her wits, thoroughly enjoyed her elevated position.

The officer was very gallant, and said all sorts of pretty things on the way, so that she blushed like a schoolgirl, and simpered after the style of coy maidens of sixty years ago.

"I say, Cory," said Pipping, "your mother seems to be a-going it."

"Well, why shouldn't she?" snarled Coriolanus.

"Oh! but it ain't *quite* the cheese," said Pipping, "at her time o' life. But, my boy, you don't understand these things."

The arrival of the soldiers in the village caused a tremendous sensation. Everybody looked frightened, and there were only women and children inside the houses.

Some of the men were seen making for the

"They go to warn Varsanta," said the officer; "but it matters not. To-morrow we will capture and hang him."

"Is that what you came for, sir?" asked Mrs. Pipping, softly.

"Yes, fair one," was the answer. "Tidings of the doings of the knave have reached the government, and we are told off to destroy him."

The carabineers took possession of the inn in the king's name, and Vampa was set free to see they were well cared for.

"No tricks, you dog!" said the officer, "or you hang. I have *carte blanche* to deal with you as I please. Prepare a good dinner for myself and my English friends."

So far all was well.

Pipping wanted a good dinner, as soon as he could get it, but he could not stand the gallantry of the man.

So he took occasion to quietly remonstrate with his spouse.

"Look here, old girl," he said, "it isn't quite right, you know. If you was to see me a-going on with a lady of high degree—"

"Oh! get out," she said.

"What?" exclaimed Pipping.

"Get out!" repeated Mrs. Pipping, deliberately. "Don't bother."

"Here, come. Do you want to see me—"

"Not likely. What lady of high degree would look at you? The thing's ridiculous."

And the bare idea of it set Mrs. Pipping laughing.

"I don't want to assert my authority as a husband," said Pipping, "but—"

"You'd better not," interposed his wife.

looked at him with quiet indifference. He gave in.

"All right," he said. "Do as you like, but draw the line."

The officer made himself one of their party, and very jolly he was, in a way. He smoked and drank rather freely—probably because he did not have to pay for anything—and he was *so* attentive to Mrs. Pipping.

At dinner he gave her all the tender bits, and helped her to wine. Towards Pipping he bore himself as a comrade.

"I have a thought," he said, as the meal concluded.

"A pretty one, I'll be bound," said Mrs. Pipping.

"My dear!" remonstrated Pipping.

"Don't be stupid!" she said.

"The thought is zis," said the officer, sipping his wine. "I am sent to direct ze destruction of Varsanta. I daren't. Pipping, ole man," clapping him on the back, "you shall do him."

"Me!" exclaimed Pipping, aghast.

"Who so good for ze job?" said the officer. "You are Englese, and you are brave. To you it shall come to attack Varsanta in his stronghold. Capture and slay him. *I* will remain here with half of ze men to protect ze lady."

"Look here," said Pipping. "I ain't a fighting man—

"Go to," the officer said, digging him in the ribs; "you, who cannot be held by Varsanta! You who escape! Ha! ha! my friend, ze sight of you shall be a terror to him. He will lie down like ze dog whipped when he see you."

"But—"

"You say—I have no arms. Well, you shall be armed. No uniform—I will get you one. Ze coat of one man who stopped behind, ze breeches of anoder, ze boots of anoder, and a hat—you are there, full, ample, a general—a commander. You shall go."

"Yes, Ribby, you must," urged Mrs. Pipping.

"Dere is no danger," said the officer. "You lead from behind and send dem on. Say to dem, 'Go, take ze castle.' It is done. Ze knocks are for dem, ze glory for you. Come, it is enough. I drink to you as a warrior, deep, togedder. Now—clink, thus."

Pipping made one more feeble attempt to get out of the job, but the pressure put upon him was too great to resist, and he yielded.

The idea of a uniform was pleasing, and, after all, there was no danger. The men would go forward and do the fighting, and the glory would be his.

"I'll tackle it," he said. "Cory, my boy, you'll take care of your mother in my absence."

"I don't want any taking care of," said Mrs. Pipping, curtly. "What do you take me for?"

"Well, you are going on a bit," said Pipping.

"And what of that?" asked Mrs. Pipping. "Can't I be a bit friendly with a kind-hearted Italian nobleman without being looked on as dirt? Pipping, you are a poor sort of creature, any way."

Pipping ground his teeth, but he said no more. He would go out and fight—die, perhaps, and then how sorry she would be.

"When am I to go?" he asked.

"You shall start at once," said the officer. "There is a moon to-night, and by its light the castle shall be stormed and taken. There is one of my men

who knows the way thither. The morrow's sun
shall shine upon your glory.

But Pipping only groaned.

CHAPTER XVIII.

AURA TO THE RESCUE—VARSANTA IS SUCCESS-FULLY DUPED.

HEN Aura came suddenly upon them, there were three men in the dungeon with Will.

Two, as we described in a previous chapter, were holding the delirious young fellow over the mouth of the old well, ready to dash him down.

The third was Luiji, standing a little back, to see that the bidding of Varsanta was performed.

The cry that burst from Aura's lips scared them all. The two men staggered a step or two back, and then dropped their burden—not down the well, but on the hard stone floor.

In a moment Aura had sprung forward, and was standing over him, ready to defend him to the last.

In her hand she held a small, bright dagger, which glittered ominously in the eyes of the cowardly brigands.

"What is it you would do?" she asked.

"Varsanta's bidding—nothing more."

"Do it, then," she cried. "Here lies your victim; but ere you cast him down take—my life."

"Lady," answered Luiji, "you are precious in Varsanta's eyes—we dare not harm you."

"Get you gone," retorted Aura, "and send him here to me."

"Lady," replied Luiji, "if we do that our necks will not be worth much. He will be mad."

"Go, anyway, from here," said Aura.

They hesitated.

"You hear?" she cried, stamping her foot.

One by one they sneaked away, Luiji last. The door stood wide open, and he laid his hand upon it with the evident intention of closing it.

Aura, as lithe as a panther, ran towards him, threatening him with her weapon.

He backed out, muttering anathemas on the heads of all womankind,

"Go to your tyrant master," said Aura, "and tell him that I want him—HERE! He will not be angry with you when you tell him that I am ready to come to terms with him for the life of his prisoner. He will understand you."

Luiji did not like his task; but something had to be done, and, bracing himself up, he hastened up to Varsanta, who was still drinking.

The brigand chief's mood had changed, and he was in a good humour. As Luiji entered he hailed him as a comrade, and bade him drink.

"Before I touch wine, chief," said Luiji, "I have something to tell you. I set the Lady Aura free, as you commanded, and then arranged for the disposal

"And he is dead?"

"No, chief. The lady, by some mischance, found her way to the well dungeon, and stopped us."

"Ha! did she dare?"

"Chief, she is a tigress; but she will be tame enough if you go to her. She is willing to treat with you for the life of the prisoner."

"Said she so?" cried Varsanta. "Then his life shall be spared—for this time. We must jockey this signorina with so much spirit. Where is she?"

"I left her with the Englishman by the well. She will not come to you. She asks for you to go to her."

"So let it be," said Varsanta. "She wants a consort. As for the Englishman, I will have him, if she wishes it, set free. Ha!—ha!—free to go until one of my good men can overtake him. If I mistake not he will be a poor traveller."

"He is a starveling and delirious," said Luiji.

Varsanta rose, and, filling a cup with wine, handed it to Luiji.

"Drink to our espousal—the Lady Aura and myself," he said.

"Happiness to both!" cried Luiji.

Varsanta, humming an air, left the chamber, and descended to the lower part of the castle. He was familiar with every corner of it, above and below, and was speedily at the appointed spot.

Aura was waiting for him just without the dungeon.

"My pretty bird," he said, "you have sent for me?"

"It was to ask you to have some pity on the Englishman," she replied.

"Your pity shall be mine. I will see with your eyes—hear with your ears. I will be as you to him."

" And the cost ?"

" Fair Aura, your heart, your love."

" Varsanta," said Aura, " before I say aught to that, act as you have said you would. Go in and look upon him with my eyes, hear his low moans of suffering with my ears, and then you will be moved to feel the pity that is in my breast."

" It shall be so," said Varsanta. " I have a tender heart, as you will find."

She drew aside, and he, bowing as he passed her, entered the cell.

He cast his eyes quickly around, and saw nothing but the yawning mouth of the well.

A suspicion of trickery flashed upon him, **and he** turned quickly.

But not soon enough to save himself.

He was only just in time to see the door sharply closed. The grating of the rusty bolts followed.

In a fit of mad fury he dashed himself against the door, and struck it with both of his clenched fists. The sound he made was answered by light laughter.

" Caged !" he hissed ; "duped by a woman. Woe to her if ever we meet again ! What ho ! my men ; your chief is in a snare. Help, there !"

He crossed over to the window, and leaped up to clutch the bars.

After two or three efforts he was successful.

Holding himself up he sent forth shout after shout ; but the dungeon was very low down in the gulch, and the sound of his voice scarcely reached the higher land above.

His cries seemed to return back to him from the rocks a few feet away, and he shouted himself hoarse without receiving an answering cry.

At last, tired out with his own weight, he let go and fell to the floor, where he lay gasping and breathing bitter vows of vengeance on the head of the girl who had successfully tricked him.

And where was Will all this time?

That, for the present, we must leave unsettled, and follow Percy in his adventures outside the castle.

CHAPTER XIX.

ROAMING IN A STRANGE COUNTRY—THE PURSUING BRIGANDS—A DESPERATE DEFENCE.

DARTING away from the brigands, Percy Winter did not run very far. It was soon apparent to him that he was not followed, and, pulling up, he reflected upon the position.

Will was still in prison, while he was free, and there lay the sting of it.

It was generous of Will to bid him seek his own safety and leave him to his fate, but it was hardly possible for him to do so.

Will had stood by him, and he would stand by Will.

What one had done the other might possibly accomplish.

"Only he is more reliable than I am," was Percy's reflection.

Then, again, there was Beppo, who had been so useful before, and might be again, if he could be found.

To find him it would be necessary to hang around the neighbourhood, at least, until daylight came again.

So Percy decided to remain, to sleep, if he slept at all, in some convenient nook close by, and early on the morrow to look out for Beppo.

It was the longest night Percy had ever known. Longer even than that he had spent in the castle on that memorable night when Will was waiting outside to rescue him.

Sleep, so often coy to those who most need it, refused to come.

In vain he closed his eyelids, and adopted all the expedients of the restless he had ever heard of. He counted fanciful sheep going through a gate, imagined running water, desperately endeavoured not to think at all—but in vain.

He was as wakeful as a creature of the night could be until the grey dawn was in the east.

Then, indeed, he could have slept.

But it would not do.

He must up and away, and, with limbs stiff and sore, he got upon his feet.

Although endowed with great physical strength and powers of endurance, the last two days and nights had taxed him severely.

Excitement is quite as exhaustive as fatigue, and at first he could scarcely drag one leg before another.

He was hungry and thirsty also, but the prospect of breakfast was too remote to be entertained for a moment.

Away to the left was the castle among the hills, to the right more hills, and before him—he had faced about—was the valley wherein lay the De Lustra farm. Why not return thither?

It was a bold thought, but in bold thoughts often lie the elements of safety.

Keeping as much as he could out of sight from the direction of the castle he retraced his steps to the farm.

Eventually he reached it without being, as he thought, observed, and in the sitting-room he found some odd morsels of food, which he stood in much need of.

A she-goat was bleating in the back-yard. She wanted milking, and Percy endeavoured to perform that operation, but with indifferent success.

He managed, however, to get sufficient milk to relieve his thirst and refresh himself.

After this he roamed about a little, and finally returned to the front room, where he sat down in a chair, just to rest awhile, and, of course, fell asleep.

From pleasant dreams of home he was aroused by a shouting outside.

Leaping up, he stared about him, bewildered for the moment; then, recovering his faculties, he walked quickly to the window and looked out.

The shouting arose from some scattered brigands, who were closing in upon the farm, but they were still far away.

It looked as if they had succeeded in tracing his movements during the previous night, and were now bent upon recapturing him.

Certain it was that they were coming thither, and to remain was not compatible with safety.

He cast a quick glance at the mantelpiece, and saw that the weapons once kept there by De Lustra had been taken away.

There was nothing in the place that would give him an adequate means of defence.

" I shall have to run from these vermin," he said, bitterly.

No time was to be lost. He left by the back-way, and set out at a smart pace for the hills.

He had covered quite a quarter of a mile of ground before a shout warned him that he was seen.

Still he ran on.

Always fleet of foot, he was, when in condition, a very fair match for the majority of running athletes.

Food and a short sleep had refreshed him, and at a pace the brigands could not hope to match he forged ahead.

His first care was to avoid the ravine, the trap into which he and Will were driven.

It soon appeared in view, and he bore away to the left, as if making for what looked like a sloping hill, easy of ascent.

But as he drew near, the face of it gradually changed.

The smooth rock became rugged—the gentle slope assumed an almost perpendicular form.

He had had some experience of mountaineering, and saw clearly that climbing it would be no child's play.

But climb it he must.

The brigands could not run him down, for he was by far the fleeter of foot, which he speedily proved.

When within easy distance of the hills he put on a sudden spurt, and rapidly widened the distance between them.

Up the first hill he climbed, pausing now and then to look back at his foes, who were foiled for the time, but not utterly defeated.

Half their number were making for an opening between the hills on his right, and he judged it led to the usual path across the mountains.

His ignorance of the country was his misfortune, and a great one, but he had a shrewd eye for landscape, and could single out a route in a strange land as well as the most experienced of travellers.

Glancing around he saw a route that he might successfully adopt in getting back to the castle. Could he traverse it unobserved?

To reach it he would have to descend an ugly bit of hill, and risk bodily injury by taking two or three stiffish downward leaps. That he resolved to do, and, after another look round, he began his journey.

. . . . . .

It was late in the afternoon when, almost worn out, he arrived at the foot of the very cliff which Will had scaled in his successful attempt to rescue him.

As far as he knew he had not been seen, and, comforted by that belief, he began his task.

Above was the opening in the wall made by Will on that great occasion. By it he might gain the castle and so be of some service to his friend.

The brigands would hardly give him credit for such daring, and his presence in their stronghold would not be suspected.

"Anyway, here goes," he said, between his teeth. Putting aside all thoughts of fatigue, he began the ascent, and, guided by the marks left on the previous occasion, he scaled the cliff with wondrous rapidity.

He was nearly at the top when a sound below attracted his attention. Turning his eyes downwards he saw half-a-dozen brigands close behind him.

Like sleuth-hounds they had fairly tracked him to the castle.

The brigands, all experienced mountaineers, were coming steadily on, with the easy air of men who were pretty sure of victory in the end.

They kept a wary eye upon him, and now and then one would take aim at him, as a sportsman does at a bird in its flight, but the cry of his comrades always checked him.

It would be a false game to shoot the goose that by-and-bye would lay golden eggs.

As he advanced, the top seemed to rise higher and higher, in mockery of his efforts to scale it ; but that was only fancy, of course. In truth, it was within measurable distance of him.

He soon gained the summit of the cliff a few yards to the left of the scene of Will's operations. On the narrow ledge of rock close to the castle he turned at bay.

Picking up a huge stone he called upon the brigands to stop.

They answered him with a shout of defiance.

"Your lives be on your own heads!" he said, as he hurled the missile at the foremost.

It struck the ruffian on the breast, and in a moment he was flying through the air, turning over and over, until he fell upon the ground below.

The stone fell almost at the same moment, and

" Dash it ! I shall be over the bridge and down in the—bottomless pit !"

The work was forced upon him, and not at all to his liking. He shuddered.

"But it must be done," he said; "their lives or mine."

He picked up another stone, and looked down.

The other brigands were sliding down the face of the cliff, seeking safety below.

"They have spoiled my game, anyhow," he said, bitterly. "I must follow them, and again seek safety in ignominious flight."

But it would not do to descend yet, so he remained to watch their performance.

To all appearance they had had enough of him for one day, as they, having reached the level ground, were hurrying round to the castle entrance.

Whether they left one on guard to watch his movements or not he could not tell, but their present plan was clear.

It would take him some time to descend the cliff, as it was necessary to be exceedingly careful, and their intention was evidently to attack him from above.

A few shots from the ramparts of the castle would decide his fate. Again Percy changed his plans.

Success is very often the outcome of audacity, and why should he not boldly enter the castle, as he originally intended?

At the worst he would only be captured and share the fate of his friend, and it was possible that in the mazes of the huge building he might elude the vigilance of his foes.

"Anyway, here goes," he said, as he stepped lightly to the hole made in the wall by Will.

He found, as he expected, that the door of the cell was open, and in a few moments he was well within the castle.

What a maze of gloomy passages it was, to be sure! And they were so much alike that he could not be certain which he had trodden before.

All he wanted at present was a safe hiding-place, for under cover of the night only could he hope to help his friend.

On a level with the cell by which he entered all the rooms were very barren, and hiding within them was impracticable, so he descended a stone staircase of about a score steps, and found himself in a big chamber, furnished with all sorts of odds and ends, doubtless the proceeds of various raids upon the homesteads around.

In one corner stood a large oaken chest. He raised the lid and saw it was empty.

"The question is, can I breathe there?" he murmured. He stepped in, and, having examined it to see that there was no spring to catch and keep him there, gently lowered the lid.

The only air opening was that of the time-worn keyhole, and by placing his mouth close to it he found that he could breathe with tolerable freedom.

"Here will I hide until darkness comes," he said. "In an hour or so it will be night."

Barely had he settled down to make the best of the situation when he heard a door open, and two or three heavy-footed men entered the chamber.

"I tell you it is so," one said; "the news comes by Paulo, who stole away from the village to warn us."

"Well, what is to be done?" asked another speaker.

"We must wait for the commands of the chief."

"He should be told."

"Luiji says we are not to seek him now; he is too deeply engaged."

"And what is Luiji doing?"

"Getting drunk with the chief's wine, and the sorry dog would not so much as moisten my lips with it."

Then they both began to growl and use language not fit for ears polite, until a third voice was heard in the doorway, crying—

"Look to it, you fellows! Here comes Luiji —drunk and mad!"

CHAPTER XX.

DODGING THE BRIGANDS—TOGETHER AGAIN— BESIEGED.

UIJI was very drunk indeed — riotously, blatantly aggressively drunk.

After the first few words he addressed to the brigands he began to abuse them and breathe threats of what he would do if they were not obedient to him.

"To you?" replied one of the men. "Why? You are only one of us."

"I am your captain!" roared Luiji; "your leader now. Varsanta has gone away on his honeymoon."

"A fig for that story," was the reply; "we are

seeking him.   That confounded Englishman who escaped us last night is in the castle."

" What—is he retaken ?"

"No—he came hither on his own account."

"A fig for *your* story," said Luiji ; "he is not such a fool !"

"Fool or no fool," rejoined the man, "he has come—as we reckon—to rescue his friend."

"Ah !" exclaimed Luiji, with drunken gravity. " I had forgotten *him*—and, let me see—something happened.   I can't remember exactly what it was just yet.   Hum ! the girl—the well—I know now. Hurry up, you dogs, or they may get away.   Follow me."

Roaring and bellowing like a bull, he hurried out of the chamber, and the others followed, to Percy's intense relief.

As soon as all was still he emerged cautiously from the oaken chest, and found that it was almost dark.   He could barely see across the chamber.

One thing he felt he must do, at all risks, and that was to see if he could find Will.

He judged rightly that in their present humour the brigands might take it into their heads to sacrifice his life ; but the puzzling question was—where was he ?

The castle was a big place, and the chances against finding Will were very great ; but thinking over the obstacles to success was not at all helpful. Percy wisely decided to act.

Opening the door, he listened for a moment, and hearing nothing but distant sounds of men moving to and fro, he passed into the passage and went boldly forward.

In a short time Percy found himself at the head

of a flight of stone steps, down which he slowly crept, groping his way by the wall.

Half-way down a narrow slit in the wall gave him a partial view of the courtyard, across which some men bearing torches were moving.

By listening closely Percy made out that the chief Varsanta had not yet been found, and he also heard Aura, her father, and Will mentioned.

But what was said precisely concerning them he could not catch.

He was about to renew his descent when he heard a slight movement below, and, standing quite still, he listened with all his ears.

Somebody was coming stealthily up the stairs.

At first he could only make out one footstep; but as the sounds drew nearer he distinguished two or three.

This was embarrassing.

He did not want to go back, but he rather suspected these stealthy footsteps were coming in search of him.

It was certain that the brigands knew he was in the neighbourhood, and had probably, by searching the rest of the castle, guessed at his exact whereabouts.

"I'll have a fight for it," said Percy, grimly, between his teeth. "When they get near enough I'll hit out, and take what follows."

He took up a firm position, and got ready for the fray in the dark.

Up came the stealthy marauders, as he thought, until they were but two or three steps beneath.

Then one of them spoke in a whisper—

"It is our only way, if you are sure you can safely descend the precipice."

"I am quite a mountaineer," answered another voice—a woman's.

The feeling of Percy was that of overwhelming astonishment.

He recognised in one speaker his friend Will— in the other, Aura !

And now a third voice was heard.

"You may trust us both. We are used to hill-work, and think nothing of it."

This was Sylvio de Lustra without a doubt.

"Hush, all of you !" said Percy, in a low, thrilling tone.   "Don't cry out. It is I—Percy. Some wondrous chance has brought us together."

Then he stopped, and, for a few moments, nothing was heard but the quick breathing of his suspicious friends. Anon the voice of Will was heard—

"It *can't* be you, Percy.   It isn't possible."

"It is not only possible but true," replied Percy, "but leave all explanations for the present. Hold out your hand."

Will extended it.

Percy found it and grasped it in the dark.

"Is that flesh and blood ?" asked Percy.

"The old grip !" replied Will, joyously.

A hurried consultation took place between them.

It seemed, from what Percy said, that the ordinary outlet of the castle was blocked by the brigands in the courtyard, and, after dodging about the place for some time they, elected to try and find the opening in the wall, and make an attempt to escape by the precipice.

"Only we are not quite certain of our way," said Will.

"I am pretty sure of it," replied Percy, "as I have quite recently entered by it."

"You be our guide then, old fellow!"

Percy turned back, and they went on in company.

Suddenly a door below was opened, and the flickering light of torches flashed up the stairs.

"I tell you," roared the voice of Luiji, "that I will have the whole place searched again and again, until I find somebody. On, you hounds—on."

The crack of a whip was next heard, and half-a-dozen men came bounding up the steps. Our friends fled onwards.

Aura and her father were placed in front, while Will and Percy assumed the rearward position, to act as defenders.

Unhappily Sylvio de Lustra was not so active as he had been in his earlier years, and the inevitable soon happened.

The more agile brigands speedily drew near enough to sight the foe.

A yell burst from their lips, filling the staircase and passage above with dismal echoes.

With a feeling akin to terror, Will urged the Italian and his daughter on.

"For your lives—hasten!" he said.

They did their best, and reached the head of the stairs, when two passages were seen by the upraised glaring light.

"Which way shall we take?" asked Aura, breathlessly.

Percy did not know. How should he, for had he not groped his way there in the dark?

He could only guess it, and he cried—

"To the right!"

And the right was wrong.

The passage was a short one, and at the bottom was an open door.

A glance, aided by the light of the advancing torches, showed that it was a furnished chamber, and a groan burst from Percy's lips.

But there was no retreat.

They had to go on and risk everything.

Into the chamber they poured, and Will closed the door.

Quickly he ran his hand down the inside and found a bolt. He drew it.

Another, and he drew that also, and both slipped into very strong sockets.

"Bring here all the furniture you can—quick !" cried Will, who added to the strength of the bolts his own weight against the door. "Oh ! for a little light."

But they had none, and the work of barricading the door had to be done in the dark.

They all did their share, while the brigands beat the door and yelled in fury, like ungovernable madmen.

"It's a strong door—that is one poor crumb of comfort," thought Will ; "but, after all, we are like rats in a cage."

It took time, but eventually they succeeded in getting some heavy pieces of furniture—a table, a chest or two, and a huge wooden settee, covered, as they could feel, with the carver's work—against the door.

So far all was well.

The barricade was an effectual one for the time.

But what of the means the brigands had for breaking it down ?

And if they could not do so were the poor friends not as much prisoners as they had been before ?

Although safe for the time, for the night, and

perchance, the morrow, they could not abide there long.

Eventually they would be starved out.

Dark—aye! very dark—was the outlook still.

CHAPTER XXI.

RIBSTONE PIPPING AS A VALIANT COMMANDER— STORMING THE CASTLE.

HE night was far spent and the day at hand.

From out of the darkness the long line of hills was slowly emerging, the tops being faintly gilded with the light of the coming sun. Down in the valley near the castle the gloom still hovered like some sullen beast in its lair. In the gloom a band of men were slowly tramping. Behind them rode a man on a mule.

The former were the carabineers, the latter was Ribstone Pipping.

He was acting the part of a prudent general by commanding from the rear.

The original intention of this party had been to attack the castle under the cover of darkness; but, thanks to some blundering, they had lost their way, and only recovered it when the first faint light of dawn revealed the outline of the castle against the sky.

Ribstone Pipping was armed with nothing more dangerous than an umbrella, which he flourished over his head, in imitation of the pictures of generals, with drawn swords, leading their men to glory.

Perhaps the fact that his soldiers did not understand a word he said had something to do with their having gone astray.

Certain it is, that whatever he said did not appear to make the least impression upon them.

Their real leader was a grim old sergeant, with an ugly scar upon his face, and a general look of having smelt powder about him.

Occasionally he said something to Ribstone Pipping which that worthy could not fathom.

Happily he could not, for it was anything but complimentary, and was, indeed, for the most part, virulent abuse. We translate a little bit of it for the edification of the reader.

"You are a pig," said the old sergeant, "and my captain is a fool for sending you with us."

"Certainly," replied Pipping, in English, "I don't think we can do better. Forward—fours, right wheel. By yer left. March!"

The men were going on in a higgledy-piggledy manner, and they continued to do so.

To them the words of command uttered by the warlike Pipping were as comprehensible as so much double Dutch.

The sergeant having further relieved his feelings by calling Pipping "a miserable beast," urged his men forward with a few more strong words and a full round oath.

As they neared the castle they expected to be challenged or fired upon, but, to their surprise, no notice was taken of them.

Nor were any sentries to be perceived upon the walls, and the only barrier visible to their entry into the castle was the huge gate closed.

So they went on, reached the bridge, and the carabineers hurriedly crossed, so as to get under the shelter of the walls.

Pipping, on his steed, followed them because his mule took him there, and as soon as it was upon the perilous elevation of the narrow bridge it began to show a frolicsome spirit.

"Whoa! you beast," roared Pipping, as it reared up; "what now?" and then it reversed the action, hoisting its hinder parts in the air. "Dash it! hang it! I shall be over the bridge and down into the — bottomless pit!"

The sergeant, who with his men had been quietly endeavouring to burst open the gate, looked fiercely round.

"Camel!" he hissed; "keep your tongue still."

"Just so," replied Pipping; "it is a most un-governable brute. Catch hold of his head."

The sergeant shook his fist at him, and Pipping, interpreting the action for the benefit of the mule, said—

"Ah! that's all very well; but a good kick in the ribs would be better physic. Come out of it! Whoa! Where are you going to?"

The mule was bent on turning round, which it succeeded in doing, after a lot of scrambling and snorting. Pipping lay full length upon its back, and with closed eyes gave himself up for lost.

The mule having got round, the half-maddened sergeant bestowed upon it a kick, which it responded to by letting out its heels.

Away went Pipping over its head, and landed on

his stomach, arms and legs extended, breathless, but saved.

Before he could get up there was a stampede of the soldiers over him, the sergeant crying—

"Run, you dromedary ! There is a bag of powder fixed on the gate, with a fuse."

Pipping did not understand him, but he knew that something was wrong, and, by a strenuous effort, succeeded in getting upon his feet.

The next moment a broad flame of light spread out before him. The mule, standing peacefully by, was violently thrown against him, and the gate, with a tremendous crash, was split in half-a-dozen directions.

A roar of alarm was heard inside, and the sergeant, snorting like a war-horse, dashed forward again.

His men followed close at his heels, and Pipping, again prostrate on the ground, was left behind.

The mule also was temporarily *hors de combat,* having been turned completely over, and it lay upon its side with its tongue lolling out and eyes staring.

Meanwhile war in earnest had begun.

Within the courtyard were half-a-dozen brigands, who, though taken by surprise by the bursting in of the gate, turned like wolves at bay upon the soldiers.

A desperate conflict ensued, in which the trained men had the advantage, and, in less time than it takes to write it, the six followers of Varsanta were dead or writhing in mortal agony upon the ground.

The old sergeant, with all his tiger instincts fully aroused, glared round in search of other foes, but seeing none, he told off four men to guard the gate, and with the rest dashed into the castle by the doorway that led to the great hall.

Nobody was there, and, thirsting for more fighting, the sergeant gazed around him with disappointed eyes.

"Is that *all* ?" he hissed. "Six—it is nothing."

"There is fighting going on somewhere," said one of the men ; " I can hear it."

"Listen !" cried the sergeant, fiercely.

They all stood still—there were about a score of them—and the sounds of a commotion above were plainly heard.

"It is there !" said one.

"No, it is there," cried another.

"Both wrong !" retorted the sergeant. "Follow me."

He darted towards a door on the left side of the hall, kicked it open, and saw ahead a stone stair-case.

Above that the commotion was going on.

There was a hammering on wood, shouting, yelling, and cries of defiance, and at last a gun was discharged.

The sergeant, with his nostrils dilated, and his already blood-stained sword well advanced, went up the stairs three at a time, and, guided by the sounds, speedily found himself confronted by two pas-sages.

The disturbance was going on in the right-hand one.

Away he went, with his panting men behind him, and, by the imperfect light which struggled through miserable little slits in the wall, beheld a crowd of brigands busy in an attempt to break down an oaken door.

It was naturally very strong, and by the sturdy re-sistance it offered appeared to be barricaded behind.

In short, it was the door of the chamber in which our friends had taken refuge.

All night long it had withstood the efforts of the brigands to break it down.

It is true they had not been quite so energetic as they might have been, for, confident of their prey, they had gone leisurely to work.

More than once they had stopped to rest, drink, and smoke; but at last, when it was too late, they were putting forth all their energies.

With only eyes and ears for what they were engaged on, they had heard nothing of the fray below, and when the carabineers threw themselves in their midst their surprise and confusion in a moment was overwhelming.

It was a short but desperate struggle.

With half their number slain, the rest threw down their arms and cried for mercy.

Then Luiji and some seven or eight of the dismayed band had their arms bound, and a few questions were put to them.

The answers satisfied the sergeant that, with the half-dozen killed in the courtyard, the defeat of the band was complete.

Only the leader was wanting, and of him Luiji vowed he knew nothing.

"He has stolen a bride," said Luiji, "and gone away on a honeymoon."

"And who is it you were unearthing?" asked the sergeant.

"Some English prisoners—confound them!" replied Luiji. "The luck at last is all on their side."

"We must set them free," said the sergeant. "Break down the door," he added, addressing his men: "but first let me hold parley with them."

This was an easy matter, for the upper part of the door had been broken in, and through it the sounds of the struggle in the passage had reached the ears of the prisoners, giving them new life and hope.

Half-a-dozen sentences were exchanged between the sergeant and Will, and then the barricade was demolished.

The door was opened, and the sergeant, with many ugly signs of the combat about him, strode into the room.

"Signors and signorina," he said, "you are safe now. We have fought for you, and the brigands are decimated. Forgive me if I am proud of this morning's work.

"It is work that you shall be well paid for," replied Percy, shaking his hand. "We have passed a terrible night—no food or rest—and this lady is exhausted."

Aura faintly smiled.

"It is enough that we are saved," she said, and, throwing her arms about her father's neck, she sobbed with excitement and joy.

CHAPTER XXII.

BACK TO THE INN—ONE THING FORGOTTEN— CAPTAIN BODABILLO SHORN OF HIS PLUMES.

AVING extracted from Luiji where the wine was kept, the cellar of the brigand was invaded, and a liberal supply for everybody taken therefrom. A few glasses to each gave new life to all.

The first natural desire of those who had known captivity in the brigand's haunt was to get away from the place, and the sergeant gave orders for their immediate retirement.

Aura was much exhausted still by the night's excitement, and was not in a condition to walk.

The sergeant remembered Pipping and his mule, and despatched one of his men for the latter.

"If the English camel objects," he said, "drop him over the precipice."

"Have you an Englishman here?" asked Will.

"One was sent with us by our mad captain," replied the sergeant, bitterly, "to lead us. Signor, he did so—from the rear."

"I should like to see this noble specimen of my countrymen," said Will.

Pipping and his mule were soon found, for as the party descended to the courtyard they appeared at the gate.

Pipping was not riding, having too much regard for his neck to voluntarily ride over the bridge. He was hauling his gallant steed by the bridle.

"Come up, you ugly beast," he was saying. "I'll knock your head off if you jib much longer. Now then, are you coming?"

"What on earth is this?" cried Percy, staring at the valiant Pipping, who, in addition to hauling at the bridle was belabouring the ribs of the mule with his umbrella.

Hearing the English tongue, Pipping wheeled smartly round.

Seeing two of his countrymen he let go of the mule, who ran off, and joyously bore down upon them.

"Prisoners, I presume," he said.

"We have been so," said Will, with a smile; "and you?"

"Oh! I was boxed up here once," carelessly answered Pipping, "but I managed to get away, and hearing of your trouble, I just come along to see if I could help you."

"On my word it is kind of you," said Will; "you are a brave fellow."

"Signors," said the sergeant, who had in a measure succeeded in interpreting what Pipping said —he was guided mainly by action—"that man is a pig—a coward—a buffoon! Why was he sent here?"

"That is what puzzles us," replied Will.

"I have a captain," said the sergeant, "a fool—a poppinjay. His name is Bodabillo. He woos every woman, and he is paying mocking attention to this pig's wife. So he was sent away."

"It's all true," broke in Pipping, in utter ignorance of all that had been said. "We've done our best, and fought and won. Hard luck to have been all night on a mule with a back like a big cross-cut saw."

"We will give you credit for having done your best anyway," said Will, good-naturedly. "Sergeant, we are ready to depart."

The mule had been caught by one of the men, and Aura having been lifted into the saddle, another glass of wine was handed round to each. With an escort, our friends, who had suffered so much within these grim walls, started for the village.

Pipping accompanied them, and on the way made much of his share in the rescue, and hinted at other deeds of valour he had performed abroad and at home.

The sergeant and two or three remained behind for awhile ; but ere a third of the journey was performed they overtook the others.

Percy thought they had remained behind for plunder, but they brought nothing with them.

"There was nothing worth the carrying," said the sergeant, in reply to a jesting question on the subject. "We stopped behind to destroy the nest."

They turned to look in the direction of his outstretched hand, and saw a huge column of smoke rising up in the morning air.

The castle had been set on fire.

"Who would have thought that the old stone place would burn ?" exclaimed Will.

"Signor," said the sergeant, "all the ceilings have rafters as dry as tinder. Trust me—it will burn. To-morrow there will be nothing but a heap of stones."

A cry escaped Aura.

Every eye was turned upon her.

"Varsanta!" she said. "I had forgotten him. I shut him up in one of the lower dungeons. I did it," she added, with a blush to Will, "shortly after I found you."

"Aura," said Will, "you have not told me all the story of the saving of my life."

"It is nothing," she said, softly.

"If Varsanta is still in one of the lower dungeons," said the sergeant, coolly, "nothing can save him. We have fired the gate. It is next to impossible to re-enter the castle."

"It is a dog's death," said Sylvio de Lustra, "and he deserves it."

"I would not doom a dog to such a death," said Will; "but we cannot help him. Let us get on."

.   .   .   .   .   .

Great was the commotion when the party returned from the mountains. The success of the expedition had been as unexpected as it was overwhelming.

It was complete.

Dismay reigned in the village—the shadow of ruin lay on Vampa's inn.

Vampa himself gave way to despair.

"They will hang us all," he said to his wife.

"May they spare Beppo," she cried.

"I care not," said Vampa, "if he hangs with us.

"He is our son," she said, reproachfully; "but you had never a heart, Vampa."

Three people in the inn heard the news with mingled emotion—Mrs. Pipping, Coriolanus, and Captain Bodabillo.

Coriolanus wondered what on earth had come to his father that he should go upon such an expedition and return victorious?

To tell the truth, this amiable son had been calculating on the decease of his father, and had already laid out certain plans for the full enjoyment of "the old man's money."

Mrs. Pipping was proud of her husband, but she had a bone to pick with him for having left her to be persecuted by that "Italian Fandango feller."

Not but what she had got the best of it, for the captain having rashly become too pressing in his attentions, she had fallen upon him in much the same way as she had descended upon Luiji in the castle.

With this difference only.

In the case of Captain Bodabillo she had been much more energetic.

He was, at the time of the return of the party, in his room, with his face bandaged, to hide the very handsome scratching record Mrs. Pipping had left upon it.

She had also removed a considerable portion of the hair of his head, and plucked out one end of his moustache.

In every way she had proved that she was a lady not to be trifled with.

The sergeant went up to his room, and, on seeing the condition of his chief, uttered an exclamation of surprise.

"Has there been fighting here, capitano?" he exclaimed, in mock dismay.

"It is that fat fiend of a woman—the wife of that barrel of a man, Pipping," replied Captain Bodabillo. "She hates me because I will not show her any attention, and last eve I fell asleep in her presence —then she set upon me."

"The vile wretch!" said the sergeant, secretly chuckling. "Wll you have her cast into prison?"

"No," said the captain, carelessly, "she is a woman. I must forgive her. Say nothing of it. For her sake I will attribute my injuries to a fall upon a cactus plant."

"Capitano," said the sergeant, "you are too noble. What are your orders?"

"Eat and drink everything in the house," replied the captain, fiercely, "and then away to Naples."

"Who goes with us besides the brigands, capitano?"

"All—a murrain on all the English! I will give them some trouble—all I can. Put the fat fiend of woman well in the rear, for I do not desire to look upon her again."

CHAPTER XXIII.

THE LAZZARONI—A GRAND PROCESSION—A DARK FACE IN THE CROWD.

CLOUDLESS day in Naples—the city of which a great writer of poetic mind said, "See it and die."

By that he meant that Naples once seen left nothing for man to care for. Nothing on earth equalled it—nothing could surpass it.

Without exactly endorsing this eulogy, we may admit that the situation of Naples is superb and the city itself a picture.

In front there lies the bay, which, on the particular day we write of, was of the deepest blue.

Behind, in the distance, turbulent, dangerous Vesuvius reared its head, a thin column of smoke rising straight into the sky in evidence that its awful fires were not as yet extinguished.

In one of the broadest thoroughfares of the city, on the steps of a handsome church, a number of beggars, called the lazzaroni, were taking their midday meal.

It was a very simple feast, consisting of a few strings of maccaroni.

Lying on their backs, the lazzaroni dropped the warm, pipe-shaped food into their mouths, gave it a bite or two, and swallowed it.

The whole thing was the very essence of laziness. The beggars were even too idle to talk to each other.

In the sun-scorched street there was very little movement.

Here and there some perspiring foot-passenger crawled along, and that was all.

Suddenly one of the lazzaroni pricked up his ears.

"Listen !" he said, softly.

"What is it ?" asked another.

"Soldiers," was the reply ; "I hear the jingling of harness and the rattle of swords. Perhaps it is the king."

Immediately, like actors who get the cue for the rising of the curtain, they one and all posed for effect, each assuming some especial position expressive of misery.

This was done on the off-chance of the king or

some of his retine taking pity on their sufferings and throwing a few coins among them.

But it was not the king.

It was our friends, with the soldiers and some of their foes, returning from the village of Palestra.

First of all came Captain Bodabillo. patched up as to the injuries he had received from Mrs. Pipping, and looking as fierce and gallant as he could under the circumstances.

Behind him, on mules, rode Percy Winter and Will Gordon, neither of them exteriorly much the worse for their recent adventures.

Next to them were Sylvio de Lustra and his daughter Aura.

Then followed half-a-dozen carabineers, succeeded by the Pipping family.

Last of all, Vampa and the captured brigands, guarded by the remnant of the band of soldiers.

The show was picturesque in many ways, if it was not so good as royalty, and there was a considerable sprinkling of Naples idlers in attendance.

As it passed along the cry of " Brigands !" was heard at different times, and some very anti-complimentary remarks were hurled at the heads of the prisoners.

While free, and pursuing their nefarious work, they were heroes ; but, now that they had been laid by the heels, they were "Dogs !" "Devils !" "Camels !" "Scaramouches !" and what not besides.

Ribstone Pipping was riding very uncomfortably ; but he felt proud of the excitement he had a share in.

The fact was, he had not quite got over his previous mule-riding, and was compelled to sit in a lop-sided way, resting on his legs in turn, instead of sitting in the customary manner, fair and square.

Mrs. Pipping was also elated, and when a little extra hullabaloo was raised by the crowd she bowed graciously like some queen or princess passing by her people.

In front of a big hotel the cavalcade was brought to a standstill.

"Halt!" cried Captain Bodabillo, reining up his steed.

Everybody halted as soon as they could ; but Ribstone Pipping, being taken by surprise, and not reining up as smartly as he ought to have done, got the head of his mule mixed up with the hind legs of a carabineer's horse.

Much lashing out and blundering about followed.

The mule got a kick in his tough chest, which made him blink and snort, and Pipping rolled out of the saddle right under the belly of the beast he had been lately riding.

"Blow the brute!" he muttered, as he hastily scrambled out. "What trick will he get up to next, I wonder?"

Captain Bodabillo, espying him from afar, called him a "pig" and bade him get up and go into the hotel.

Will and Percy, with De Lustra and his daughter, had already gone up the steps into the building

"What did he call you, Ribby?" enquired Mrs. Pipping.

"A pig," replied Pipping.

"Are you a man to stand that?" demanded Mrs. Pipping. "Why don't you go for him?"

"Go for—how?" asked Pipping, feebly.

"Go up to him and ask what he means by it," replied Mrs. Pipping. "You've told me how you used to fight when you were a boy. Don't give in now you're a man."

"All right," said Pipping, "here's at him."

Putting on as manly a stride as he could under the circumstances, he strutted up to the gallant captain, who had just dismounted and given his horse to the care of an orderly.

"You called me something?" said Pipping.

"Yes," said the captain, coolly; "a pig."

"Then let me tell you," rejoined Pipping, "that you are a—a porker."

"A what?" demanded Captain Bodabillo, fiercely.

"A porker," said Pipping; "young swine—and not dairy fed."

"Ha!" exclaimed Bodabillo, putting his hand upon his sword.

"Come, none o' that," said Pipping. "Fight like a man. Up with your fists. Now then, I'm on."

Pipping began to dance and spar in the most scientific manner. "One, two, three—upper cut!"

As Pipping spoke he darted in and delivered an upper cut to the fiery captain, who, unaccustomed to that mode of warfare, received it without making any attempt to defend himself.

Any sort of upper cut is bad, and the wretched captain was sent staggering back, speechless with agony.

Pipping did a short war-dance in his neighbourhood, and then retreated up the steps.

"If you want any more of it," he said, defiantly, "you know the shop to come to."

"Ribby," said Mrs. Pipping, panting up the steps, "I shall look upon you as a *man* from this hour."

"Pig, beast, brute, fool!" gasped Captain Bodabillo. "I make you for zis dead, cold meat. Remember, beware!"

"Pooh!" contemptuously replied Pipping, "you don't scare me. Jane, take my arm. Let us enter this 'ere place as if we were somebody."

Leaving Bodabillo foaming and threatening, they entered the hotel.

"Oh! my," exclaimed Mrs. Pipping, looking round the hall, "ain't it gorgess."

"Hush! don't let 'em see you ain't used to it."

"But won't it come expensive, Ribby?"

"Yes—yes, but Mister Winter's going to lend me a bit till I can write home. It's all right. Come on. Garshong, la private room, two to sleep in, and a bottle of wine after that ride. I'm grilled with thirst."

Meanwhile Percy and Will had parted with Aura and her father, and been shown to a double-bedded room to indulge in the luxury of a wash after their long ride.

"I say, Percy, said Will, as he poured out some water into the basin, "as we came along just now did you notice a crowd at the corner of the street?'

"I did," answered Percy, "but not particularly."

"Well, did you see a face you know—a dark-looking, swarthy face?"

"I did and recognised it."

"Who was it?"

"Either Varsanta or his twin brother," coolly replied Will, as he began his ablutions.

CHAPTER XXIV.

PERCY GOES FOR A SAIL—A STRUGGLE IN A
BOAT AND A STRANGE SWIM WITH A SERIOUS
FINALE.

EVER—impossible !"
exclaimed Percy.

Will gave himself
a good sluicing be-
fore replying, and
when he was towel-
ing himself, he
said—

"It's a fact, old
fellow. It was Var-
santa. He *couldn't*
have a twin bro-
ther. The world
could not hold two
such scoundrels."

"But the brute was buried under the castle at
Palestra."

"He wasn't, it appears. Somehow he managed
to get out."

It was unsatisfactory, anyway.

Not only was the brigand free to work more
mischief, but it was disappointing that a just punishment had not overtaken him.

"But why should he come to Naples?" asked
Percy.

"Does not nearly every provincial knave in the
old country at home make tracks for London?"
answered Will.

It was an accepted fact Percy could not controvert.

" I hoped," he said, "that we had done with him for good and all, and I shall not rest until I have seen the end of that villain, Varsanta."

If they could they would have kept the matter from Aura and her father, but with the brigand at large it would be dangerous for them to go abroad without an escort after nightfall.

A warning to them was therefore imperative.

Will Gordon, for reasons which will be understood, appointed himself to the position of escort.

Percy was then left very much to himself, and having no particular taste for the society of Ribstone Pipping, who, with the money advanced to him, was "seeing the sights" of Naples, he, during the next few days, often went out alone.

In a short time the trial of the brigands would take place, and the whole of the party had received notices to attend as witnesses.

To ensure their attendance the chief of police had temporarily suspended their passports.

At times, when Percy was abroad, he felt convinced that his footsteps were being dogged, but as he prudently avoided the low quarters of the town he had nothing to fear.

One day, roaming about by the sea, two boatmen accosted him.

"English sar," they said, "haf boat—good boat."

Resting with one end lightly upon the shore was one of those slim craft with a latteen sail so dear to the Neapolitan heart.

Percy had heard much of the wonderful sailing powers of these craft, but had never been out in one.

It would while away an hour to test their qualities, so he stepped in.

Of the boatmen he took very little notice, but a more sinister-looking pair of ruffians never sailed a boat in the lovely bay.

As soon as Percy had taken his seat they pushed off, stepped in, and hoisted the huge sail.

The breeze was light, but the boat skimmed over the gently rocking sea like a bird, so that Naples was soon a mile or more behind.

There were few other boats in the bay, for it was the hour of noon, when most of the inhabitants and visitors preferred the shade to sunshine.

Percy sat near the bow of the boat thinking. The boatmen, in the stern, watched him closely, occasionally exchanging a few words in a whisper.

Suddenly looking up, Percy caught the two men staring at him with an evil light in their eyes.

It flashed upon him then that they meant mischief.

"I think you have gone far enough," he said, quietly. "Put about, and make for home."

"Signor," replied one of the men, "it is zo impossible. Ze breeze. Vind vill not permit."

"You do as I tell you," cried Percy, hotly; "put about."

A few more words, in some *patois* unknown to Percy, were exchanged by the men, and then one sullenly arose and came forward.

When near Percy he stooped as if to loosen the sail; but, instead of doing so, he whipped a knife out of his belt and raised his hand to strike.

Percy saw the movement in time, and, springing up, closed with him.

The second man also leapt up, and, raising the

oar he had used for steering, aimed a blow at Percy's head.

The struggling shifted the positions of Percy and his foe, and the consequence was that the fellow struck his companion, who, with a groan, fell upon the leeward side of the boat.

His weight, and the fact of the other two being erect, and on that side also, brought about a catastrophe.

The boat upset, and, rapidly filling, went down, leaving Percy and his foe in the water.

Like a leaden plummet the man who had been struck went down under the sea.

His companion, with wild alarm in his eyes, struck out for the shore.

Percy was a splendid swimmer; but the struggle with the would-be assassin, though short, had been so fierce that he had to be content to paddle gently about for a few moments to recover his breath before making full exertions to save his life.

When he fairly started the boatman was some distance ahead of him.

"I must be first ashore," thought Percy, "and charge him with wilful murder, or he may endeavour to fix something on me."

Fortunately the clothes he was wearing were very light, and scarcely impeded his movements.

Therefore he was able to cleave the water with his strong arms almost as well as if he had been in simple bathing attire.

The boatman ahead was conscious of being pursued, and being a good swimmer also, the race was a close one. But Percy gained ground.

Steadily he drew up inch by inch until there was only a few feet between them.

The shore then was not two hundred yards away.

Pretty well pumped, and conscious of being fairly overhauled, the boatman turned upon his pursuer, and, drawing a knife, made for him.

Percy steadied himself, and swam a little slower. Then, as the boatman came up, with murder in his eyes, he suddenly stopped, lowered his legs and, "treading water," as swimmers say, hit out fair and square with his clenched fist.

So unexpected was this movement that the boatman received the blow full in the face, and, turning over, rolled under the sea.

Percy coolly resumed his swimming, and in a short time landed on the beach a little way from the city.

There was no movement ashore, and the incidents we have recorded were not apparently observed.

Percy, after a glance round, and finding all quiet, sauntered back slowly, so as to give the sun time to dry his clothes before he reached his hotel.

"I don't think I will make a song about this business," he said, with a faint smile. "Of course, I am sorry for the villains, but they brought it upon themselves. I wonder who set them on? Could it have been Varsanta?"

CHAPTER XXV.

THE ROGUES' HAUNT—VARSANTA IN HIDING— RIBSTONE PIPPING IN A TERRIBLE FIX.

IDING behind a heap of stones upon a slope, not far from the spot where Percy landed, was Varsanta the brigand.

Not only had he instigated the attempt on Percy's life, but he had been in hiding to see it carried out.

Prowling on the outskirts of the city, he saw our friend strolling about, and knowing his men, he communicated with the boatmen, and offered them a good reward if they succeeded in luring Percy into their boat and disposing of him.

"Do it your own way," he said, "but do not fail."

Having given them a few golden pieces on account, he stole away.

As we have seen, the plan rapidly conceived was doomed to ignominious failure.

The men took the price of their intended crime and their lives to the bottom of the bay.

So far, well—for Percy; but to Varsanta it was gall and wormwood.

He cared not for the lives of the boatmen. The "dogs," having bungled in their work, in his eyes

It was the fact that Percy had once more escaped that was so bitter.

With a brow black as midnight, he stole to the back of the city, and entering it by a narrow, seldom used thoroughfare, went stealthily through a number of byeways until he reached a low-class wineshop in a blind thoroughfare.

It had all the appearance of a rogue's haunt, and such, indeed, it was.

Entering the open door, he reached a dirty place which served at once as public-room and bar.

There a burly man, with a dark, ill-favoured face, was sleeping behind the counter, and in a corner on a rush settle sat two ragged, villainous-looking fellows, who were also wrapt in slumber.

The hour for the midday siesta had not yet expired.

Without heeding the sleepers, Varsanta passed into a room at the back, which he entered with a cat-like step.

Half-a-dozen other men were there, four asleep and two playing cards.

To the latter he addressed himself, speaking in the abrupt tone of offended authority.

"Why are you idling here?" he said. "Do you remember the work I set you to do?"

"Signor Varsanta," replied one of the men, "it is useless to go out to shoot cock-pigeons when every bird is in its nest."

"The English do not regard the hour of siesta," replied Varsanta. "Confound your gambling! Put away those cards."

The men, somewhat sullenly, complied, and rose to leave the room, but the brigand bade them sit down again.

"It is useless to go out now," he said ; "wait until night. Remember that as soon as you have destroyed *all* my foes the treasure is yours."

"It is to be hoped that we shall be able to find it," replied one of the men, grimly.

"Hark ye," said Varsanta, "if you doubt my word, give up the job. There are a thousand men in Naples who will do it—at the price."

"We do not doubt your word," said the man ; "by the saints, no ; but we cannot help thinking that you brought precious little away with you."

"Would you—hungry and thirsty as I was, after many long hours in a dungeon, and with enemies not far away—have lingered there?" fiercely demanded Varsanta. "Did I not suffer in that place all the terrors of a living tomb, and when the burning castle fell, breaking open the door of my prison and leaving me a narrow, dangerous way to creep out of the ruins, was I less than a man to creep out as well as I could and get away?"

"Ah! yes ; we might have done the same," said the man.

"I tell you," said Varsanta, hotly, "that it was a simple miracle that I am not still there, buried alive. The stones and rafters fell so as to leave a narrow winding way for me to crawl through the wreck of my home, and the treasure is buried now ; all you want is for me to describe the place, and it is yours. You are unknown there, and will pass over the mountains unquestioned. You will go there poor and return rich, with your pockets filled with gold.

The eyes of the men flas ed as Varsanta, in his cunning, thus described what good luck was in store for them—if they only did his bidding.

As for the treasure under the castle ruins, tha. was a myth, and if it had been there no two men, without something more than simple tools, could have dug it out in a year.

But he did not stick at trifles when he had an end in view.

If lies would help his cause he was ready to pour them out without stint.

"Understand me," he said ; "ALL these English people must *die*.   But first the two young braggarts who have been the principal cause of the breaking up of my band."

"It has been well broken up," remarked one of his hearers, grimly.

"What of that ?" savagely demanded Varsanta. 'Can I not form another ? Are there not good men ready to be led to wealth and comfort?   I tell you my castle was a Paradise !   Drink and ease and the luxuries of the rich all the year round, and sometimes only one day's work in the week to be done.   Oh ! it is a rare life—a rare life."

In this way Varsanta, not for the first time, fired the imagination of the men he wished to make tools of.

Sitting down by the rough deal table, he took a piece of chalk which had been used to draw some gambling diagram of the " shove-halfpenny " description, and roughly sketched out the elevation of the hotel.

"See here," he said ; "this is the room in which one of those accursed Englishmen sleep. You can gain access to it by climbing to the balcony.   Here, to the right, De Lustra sleeps ; the next room is his daughter's.   The pig Pipping can

friendly chat with him before I finish his business. His wife I leave to you—shoot her, hang her, drown her, just as you please. Also the boy. All *I* want is my Pipping. Gagged and bound, he can be brought here, and the cellar below is ready to receive him."

"Signor Varsanta," said the men, "you may consider it done. But we must catch our bird after dark."

"Catch him when and where you please," replied Varsanta ; " only bring him here."

Now it must be understood that the gallant Pipping knew nothing of Varsanta's escape.

Will had warned him to be careful to avoid evil company, and then let the matter rest.

There was still the possibility of his having been mistaken, that it was not considered desirable to create unnecessary alarm.

That night Ribstone Pipping walked abroad alone.

A slight tiff with his wife, who was maliciously supported by her beautiful son, sent him out in a huff

" I'll stand no more of it !" he muttered, as he strode down the steps of the hotel. "If you put up with a woman's nonsense you may be trodden on like a worm."

Ribstone Pipping had a double design in leaving the hotel.

He wished to show his manly spirit to his wife, and he also designed to go on the spree.

Not that spreeing had ever been much in his line, for all his life he had been a business-like, sober

Why should he not enjoy himself?

"I'll go to a café and have a dance," he said.

Cafés, where there is dancing after dark, are not by any means scarce in Naples, and the wild Pipping soon found one, from whence poured the seductive strains of a very fair band.

Having been charged double fee at the entrance, and paid it for the want of knowing better, he entered.

What a gorgeous sight!

Such pretty dames and gallant gentlemen dancing; promenading or sitting down at the side tables, drinking and flirting.

Ribstone Pipping thought it was a veritable fairy land.

Close by a lady in a blue silk dress was seated at a table—alone.

Pipping thought he might as well go ahead and strike up an acquaintance.

Dropping into a seat opposite her, he said—

"Uncommon fine evening, ain't it?"

The lady glanced at him quickly, then turned her head away.

"Don't be afraid o' me," said Pipping; "I'm a married man, and know how to treat a pretty gal when I see one.   Shall we have a little wine? No! don't go."   The lady had half risen, but Ribstone Pipping, leaning across the table, laid hold of her arm.

At that moment a little Italian gentleman, of middle life, drew near, with an ice in either hand.

Seeing Pipping taking this unwarrantable liberty, he dropped the ices and went for him.

"Signor," he said, giving him a fierce push, "that lady is my wife."

Pipping did not understand him, but he comprehended the nature of the attack, and dealt a sweeping round-arm blow in return.

His fist collided with the side of the Italian's head, who was sent sprawling.

The exact nature of events which followed Ribstone Pipping never clearly knew.

All he could remember was that all the men in the place, headed by a ring of *garçons*, suddenly fell upon him, and threw him out into the street.

There, to his surprise, he was picked up by some men outside, who, without any ceremony, proceeded to drag him down the street.

"Here—help — murder — drop it!" he cried.

A cloak was thrown over his head, and a cord passed round his chest, confining his arms.

He tried to cry out again, but nearly choked himself. There was not enough air to permit of a shout.

"What is this game?' he groaned. "Here, none of your larks. Let me out!"

But there was no joking in the matter.

Rapidly he was borne along through half-a-dozen streets, and then there was a sudden stop.

After that he felt himself being carried downstairs, a door was opened, and he was thrown like a bundle of rubbish into some place.

Then the door closed, bolts were drawn, and he was left to his reflections.

The feelings of Ribstone Pipping were of the most agonising description.

In addition to having been torn away from his friends and cast into some unknown place, he was bound and most effectually blindfolded.

As he did not possess much natural courage, a

thousand fears, founded and unfounded, increased the misery of his position.

The stifling air he was obliged to breathe was overpowering, and there was a possibility of his shortly succumbing to it.

———

CHAPTER XXVI.

VARSANTA'S TRIUMPH—THE RESULT OF A KICK.

HAPPILY Ribstone Pipping was relieved from the danger of suffocation by the arrival of that arch-villain, Varsanta.

The brigand came into the cell with a lantern, and having taken the precaution to lock the door and put the key into his pocket, he removed the cloak from Ribstone Pipping's head.

The moment the hapless prisoner saw who it was that had him in his power, he uttered a loud cry and nearly swooned away.

"Ha!" cried Varsanta, derisively, "you did not expect to see *me?*"

"I thought you were dead!" gasped Pipping.

"Dead!" said the brigand, scornfully. "It would take a thousand English vermin to destroy me, even if I met them single-handed."

spirit, "that I know one or two who, without help, would give you the knock."

"Bah! Who are they—what are they?"

"Jem Mace, for one."

"Jemmace!" exclaimed Varsanta. "I know him not!"

"A good job for you," replied Pipping. "And I could name a dozen others if I could look up the sporting papers. I am not a fighting man, so can't call 'em to mind."

"Now," said Varsanta, sharply, "to business. Are you prepared to die?"

The heart of Pipping throbbed violently, and the blood, first rushing into it, retreated and left him deadly pale.

"I—I think not," he said. "Not many men are."

"Well," said Varsanta, "you are going to die—not swiftly, but by inches. I am told that it was you who led the attack upon my castle. Is it true?"

"I led it—in a way," replied Pipping. "I came up behind on a beastly mule."

"Enough!" said Varsanta. "You were there. Now for my revenge. See here!"

He flourished a dagger before his victim's eyes, grinning at him like a fiend.

"How do you like it? Is it to your taste—eh?"

As he spoke he pricked Pipping with the dagger twice upon his leg.

The little man winced, but he set his teeth, and said—

"You are a cur! Just loosen my arms, and I'll give you what for!"

It was something he could not remember having felt before.

"You defy me, you Englese dog?"

"Yes, you Italian cat—you bundle of maccaroni! Ha! at it again."

Now, although Pipping's arms were bound, his legs were free—a fact Varsanta for the moment must have forgotten.

Anyway, he got just into the right position to receive a kick from the prostrate man, and Pipping gave him one that, for the time, fairly settled him.

It caught him on the side of the face, just under the ear, and knocked, or, to be more correct, kicked him out of time.

The brigand, with a sputtering cry, staggered and fell upon his side, where he lay to all appearance helpless.

In the act of falling he dropped his dagger, and Pipping, with all his wits wonderfully on the alert, rolled over and grasped it.

With its keen edge the severing of the rope around him was a matter of moments, and, elated with the prospect of escape, he sprang to his feet.

Varsanta still lay upon the ground, feebly moving his limbs, and giving out curious clucking sounds as if some clockwork inside him had got out of order.

Pipping's first care was to get the key of his prison, which, it may be here explained, looked like an old-fashioned stone cellar.

Pipping called to mind that he had heard the door locked on the inside. The key was not there, and Varsanta must have it in one of his pockets.

Thus reassured, Ribstone Pipping, with the

dagger held ready for action, proceeded to examine the brigand's clothes.

"If he moves, or tries any tricks," hissed Pipping, "I'll kill him. I've never done such a thing before, but I'll do it now."

He had never felt so determined and venomous in all his life. No doubt if Varsanta had returned to consciousness he would have killed him.

But there was no need for such an extreme measure, which was quite out of Pipping's ordinary course of life, and, having found the key, he let himself out of the cellar with all speed, and, for his own safety, locked the brigand in.

Thus was Varsanta for the second time shut up by a weaker being in a prison of his own providing.

Pipping had taken the precaution to bring the lantern with him, and by its light he found himself in a damp passage of fair width, along which was strewn packing-cases, empty bottles, straw, and other lumber common to public-houses and inns at home and abroad.

There was a door at the top-end, which he cautiously approached, and found to his joy that it opened upon a flight of steps leading to the street above.

Pipping lost not a moment in getting to the level ground, and found himself in a deserted, blind street which he had never, to his knowledge, set eyes upon before.

As there was only one road out of it he naturally took that way, and, with the dagger concealed in his pocket, he hurried through the low quarter of the town, unheeded by the few people who were abroad.

He had one guide to help him on his way.

On the left he occasionally caught a glimpse of the crown of Vesuvius, illuminated by a faint, fiery glow.

For days it had given indications of a possible eruption, but, according to the inhabitants, there was no immediate danger to the villages built upon its slopes, and none at all to Naples.

"She will shoot up a few stones and ashes, just to relieve her burdened breast," they said, "and then she will be quiet again."

By many devious ways Pipping at last got into a street he knew, and then the way to his hotel was easy.

He arrived there just as the clocks were on the point of striking twelve.

With the elasticity of a boy he bounded up the staircase, burning to tell his wife the story of his recent peril and bold escape.

He naturally expected to find a woman of her sober leanings in bed, and went straight to the room where they enjoyed repose.

Before he could enter—indeed, his fingers had only just clutched the handle—the door was opened, and an outraged wife, in her nightcap, stood before him.

"Mister Pipping," she said, "you are a low, degraded, dissipated, worthless creetur. Take that!"

"That" was a box on the ear that sent him staggering back into the lobby. The door was closed with a bang, and the click of the lock followed.

in my life. First with that thief Varsanta, and now with— Well, she's a changed woman, and I am, in a connubial sense, done for."

———

CHAPTER XXVII.

DOGGING THEIR FOOTSTEPS—THE MIDNIGHT ASSASSIN—A FAILURE.

THAT night about eight o'clock, Percy joined his friends at the theatre. Afterwards they had supper at a *café*, and strolled back to the hotel. Will and Aura were sufficiently wrapped in each other not to notice anything around them, but Percy, who walked behind with Sylvio de Lustra, had more time to look about him.

Ere they had gone far he felt almost sure that they were being shadowed by a man whose ostensible calling was that of a match-seller to the public.

Unlike the majority of these poor venders of a common necessity, he was a tall, brawny, well-fed ruffian, with a slouch hat drawn over his eyes, and a long cloak about his shoulders.

All the way back he was, more or less, in their immediate vicinity, and near the hotel he was so close to Percy that the latter turned upon him, and, in Italian, asked him what he wanted.

The man thrust his right hand quickly under his cloak—he carried the boxes of matches in his left—and replied—

"Nothing, signor. I only sell matches."

"You have been dodging about us for some time,"

The man scowled at him, and vanished with a celerity that proved the potency of the threat.

De Lustra shrugged his shoulders as they walked up the steps.

"That fellow," he said, "should be a brigand."

"He was up to no good," replied Percy, quietly. "Probably he intended to pick our pockets."

In a short time all had retired to their respective rooms. Percy and Will did not, as they had often done, occupy a double-bedded apartment, but had separate chambers.

Percy accompanied Will to his room, and told him of his suspicions about the match-seller.

"We have a gang set upon us, that is clear," he said, "and I think you ought to go away with De Lustra and Aura."

"And leave you to encounter all sorts of perils alone," returned Will.

"I can take care of myself."

"Aura ought to go," said Will, thoughtfully, "but whither? They are very poor, but as proud as Lucifer."

"I have a post to offer De Lustra," said Percy, with a smile. "I want a secretary, and he is just the man. He shall be sent to England to look into some business matters for me."

"Can he go? Remember, we are requested to remain here."

"I think we can arrange it by seeing the English Ambassador. As for ourselves, we are not going to show these bravos the white feather."

"Certainly not."

They bade each other Good-night, and Percy went to his room, where he first put out the light, then drew up the blind to enjoy the scene without.

A brilliant moon was shining in the sky, silvering all that came within the range of its rays. The opposite houses exhibited no sign of life, save here and there a light in an upper window, and the street was untenanted.

Stay! What is that across there—in the shadow?

" Surely it is the figure of a man ?" thought Percy.

He watched closely, and presently saw the form emerge out of the gloom and dart across the street.

Then the moonlight fell upon him, and Percy recognised the well-remembered figure of the match-seller.

What could he be doing there ?

Mischief of some sort was afloat.

The main entrance to the hotel was by that time closed, and there was also a night watchman on guard. Very little was to be apprehended from that direction.

But might not there be some way by which he could get into the hotel, and, when there, what would he attempt to do ?

Murder or rob ?—perhaps both.

Percy was working out these probabilities in his mind when a slight scratching on the stonework outside fell upon his ear.

Somebody was climbing the balcony just outside the window of his room.

His resolution was instantly taken.

He had a revolver in his drawer, which he quietly took out ; then, whipping off his coat and tossing it down in a conspicuous place, he lay down on the bed, drew the counterpane over his body, and feigned slumber.

Shortly after he heard a slight, grating sound at

the window, and as it slowly opened, forced by a skilful hand, the cool night breeze was wafted across his face.

A short silence followed.

Then the form of the match-seller, now without his cloak, appeared at the opening, rising up slowly, and two dark eyes scanned the chamber.

Percy drew a long, deep breath. His feigning of sleep was admirable.

Inch by inch the assassin thrust one leg into the room, and sat for a few moments upon the window-sill.

Percy, with one eye just a wee bit open, continued his sham slumber.

Under the counterpane his right hand grasped the revolver, cocked and ready for action.

Into the room, with no more sound than a cat would have made, advanced the assassin.

Crouching, step by step, he came round the bed.

And then, when he came to striking-distance, he drew himself up and raised his arm.

"Well, my friend," said Percy, pointing the revolver at his head, " what do you want ?"

The surprise was so great that the assassin stood transfixed—immovable.

Percy slipped out of bed.

" Drop that knife !" he said.

The man mechanically did as he was told.

" Sit there !"

The staggered wretch slowly stepped back and dropped into a chair Percy pointed at.

"Don't move, unless you wish to be shot like a dog," said Percy, as he stepped quietly to the bell

In a couple of minutes or so a knock was heard at the door.

"What is the matter, signor? Are you ill?"

It was the night-watchman, who was told to come in, and in his turn received a bit of a shock.

"Summon the gendarmes," said Percy. "This fellow came in through the window with the intention of assassinating me."

"The thief!—the pig!" exclaimed the night-watchman.

"Hurry up!" said Percy. "I will see that he does not get away. Pick up that knife on the floor—it will be wanted in evidence against him."

The night-watchman took possession of the weapon, and departed to summon a gendarme to take charge of the assassin.

Percy, left alone with the foiled villain, drew up a chair near him and sat down.

"For the love of all the saints," said the wretch, "let me go."

"That would be a fool's trick," replied Percy.

"I will tell you who set me on."

"That will be no news, and will not save your own hide."

"Signor, I am a poor man; I have a wife and family. I had no work, and wanted bread. Varsanta said to me, 'If you want money, earn it by killing my enemy.' I was tempted, and I fell."

"Cease your whining—it will not save you," returned Percy. "I am going to give you all the law allows for this affair. Silence!"

The fellow said no more, but sullenly awaited his fate.

He would suffer as it was, but if he attempted to get away that weapon might bark and bite him unto death.

Ah! it was better to keep still.

When the footsteps of the gendarmes—there were two of them—were heard, the assassin cast a quick glance about him, as if in search of some way of escape, but he found none, and soon the "steel braclets" were about his wrists.

"Shall I come and charge him?" asked Percy.

"It is enough that he has been found here with a knife," was the reply; "but you must come to-morrow."

Percy slipped some money into the speaker's hand, and the prisoner, with his head hanging on his breast, was taken away.

It was all done so neatly, and with so little noise, that none of the sleepers in the place were disturbed.

Percy closed the door and walked to the window, where he leant upon the sill and watched the prisoner crawl down the street between the two officers.

"A good finish to rather a lively day," he said. "Now I think I may undress and get into bed."

Five minutes later he was sound asleep.

H ! signor, there is a disturbance in the cellar. May I go down and see what it is?"

The speaker was a wild-eyed Italian girl, the servant of the inn.

She asked this question at the door of her master's bedroom, after tapping.

"Away, wench !" he cried. "Have I not told you that you were not to concern yourself with anything going on there?"

"But, signor, the noise is great—awful. It has been going on half the night."

"Go to the room where Varsanta sleeps," growled the innkeeper ; "tell him of it."

The girl went away, and in a few minutes returned again, tapping at the door.

"Furies ! who is there now? Am I to get no sleep?"

"Signor, the guest Varsanta is not there. His bed has not been slept on."

"What a fool to go out and leave a prisoner on my hands !" muttered the landlord, as he rolled out of bed ; "and such orders, too. Nobody but himself to go near the man. I wonder who it is."

Varsanta had not confided anything to the land-lord. He simply told him he wanted the use of his cellar to keep a prisoner in for a few days, and he would be the gaoler.

The men employed in capturing Ribstone Pipping had left, and one, as we have seen, had been laid by the heels in attempting to take the life of Percy Winter. What, therefore, could that landlord do but wait for the return of Varsanta.

And the brigand was below, trembling with rage like a fiend, and calling for help in vain.

There were intervals of silence, of course, for the human voice cannot be kept going at a high pitch for ever. Such intervals were a boon to the land-lord; but barely would he have began to feel at ease when Varsanta would begin again.

The matter soon assumed a very serious aspect.

At an early hour stragglers began to enter the wine-shop, and in spite of the cellar door being kept closed and muffled, the noise reached the customers' ears.

"Ah! friend," said one, "you have somebody ill here."

"It is a dog I am taking care of for a friend," sullenly replied the landlord.

"A dog? He barks very strangely!"

"I can't help that. If you think you can alter the tone of his barking go down and do it. He is as big as a mule."

Of course the customer refused to do so, and after drinking his wine went away wondering.

By-and-bye another customer came in, and in the midst of drinking a flagon of cheap wine was startled by a most unearthly howl from somewhere

"St. Sebastian !" he cried, as he dropped the flagon.   " What is that ?"

"A dog—a dog," replied the landlord ; "he is chained, and does not like it ; but he is too savage to be allowed about alone."

" I would shoot a dog like that," said the man, with a scowl; "spoiling a man's drinking with his fiendish howling."

Matters went on in this way until about eleven o'clock, when the landlord felt that he must do something, or get into trouble.

People were getting curious about that room below, and there was a band of idlers outside, discussing the subject in an undertone.

"If Varsanta is not back in half an hour," he muttered, " I'll go down and silence that dog."

Varsanta did not return, as he was himself the dog, and the landlord was now worked into a furious state.

At least half-a-dozen customers were in the wine-shop all anxious about the strange animal in the cellar.   Two or three were anxious to see it.

"You shall," said the landlord, " when he is quieter."

With the grim determination to silence the prisoner at all risks, he armed himself with a stout stick and in a white heat hastened below.

A glance at the door showed him the key out-side, just where Ribstone Pipping had left it, and turning it savagely, the landlord entered the cell.

Coming, as he had recently done, from a strong light, he could only imperfectly see objects in the cell, and when the maddened Varsanta rushed at him he dealt him a tremendous blow that stretched

he lay quite still. The landlord bent over him to
see if he were breathing, and then he saw who it was.

"Varsanta!" he gasped, as he staggered back.

Scarcely crediting that it could be the brigand
chief, he took a second look at him, which set all
doubts at rest.

"It IS Varsanta!" he gasped. "In the name of
the saints how came he here?"

This was a problem he could not solve without
the aid of Varsanta, and the probabilities of what
would happen when he came to appalled the dismayed man.

The brigand chief was not dead.

He was breathing heavily, and, in the ordinary
way, would be but temporarily insensible.

What was to be done?

The very name of Varsanta had been a terror to
certain people. By the simple force of his person-
ality he had long held the ruffian world of Naples
and the adjacent country in awe.

There was only one way of escaping his vengeance,
and that was to betray him to the authorities.

It was a desperate expedient, which would
practically shut him out from a large circle of
congenial spirits; but it was better than being shot
by the infuriated brigand.

"I'll do it!" he said.

Lying near the fallen man was the severed rope
which, for a while, had held Ribstone Pipping's
arms in its knotted embrace. He took it up,
fastened the pieces together, and tied the wrists of
the insensible brigand.

His next step was to leave the cell, secure the
door, and hurry up to the room above.

have silenced the dog," he said. "He won't bark so loud again to-day."

Then, calling his wife to take charge of the bar, he put on his hat and left the place.

Five minutes later he was in the district office of the gendarmes, making a tremulous communication to the officer in command.

"But how comes it," asked that functionary, "that this notorious villain is in your house?"

"He came and asked for a hiding-place, using threats against my life if I refused," was the reply.

The story was a probable one, and it was accepted. Half of the best men, with their commanding officer, returned with the landlord to secure the notorious brigand chief, who was supposed to be dead.

They found him just awakening from his stupor, and the sight of the gendarmes thoroughly awoke him to the perilous nature of his position.

He saw that in addition to being hoodwinked by a man he looked upon as a fool, he had been betrayed by one he considered was a friend.

His rage was not very assertive, but rather of the quiet and intense order.

"I am not dead yet," he said, as they manacled his hands and raised him up. "Ah! my friend you need not skulk there. I have eyes at such a time as this which will pierce stone walls."

He addressed the landlord, who was skulking outside the cellar, not daring to go away without leave from the gendarmes, and naturally anxious to avoid the eyes of the man he had betrayed.

"It was your own fault," he said. "You roused the whole place with your howling."

"Ah! yes," said Varsanta, slowly, "I have. You

have betrayed me. Let it be so. But, understand, I am not dead yet. We shall meet again. Gentlemen, I am at your service. Have we far to go?"

"Not far," briefly answered the officer.

"Then I will walk," said Varsanta. "Had it been otherwise I would have ridden, as becomes a man of my rank. No, I am not dead yet—not dead yet."

Muttering this, and with his eyes fixed ahead, he stalked out of the dismal cellar, with his watchful guardians in close attendance upon him.

. . . .

Popularity is a fickle thing.

The hero of to-day may be the outcast of to-morrow, and so Varsanta discovered.

Already the news of his capture had got abroad, and when the party reached the street a host of people had assembled to give him such welcome as he deserved.

When he appeared a howl of derision saluted him, dirty fists were shaken in the air, and there was a cry to kill him.

The brigand curled his lip scornfully, and turned a bold face upon the yelling people—no easy thing to do when they are of the class a man looks to for popularity.

"Hasten, there !" cried the officer, who knew the dangerous nature of the community around.

Although some might have felt a momentary indignation, there were many who might desire to aid him to escape.

With three gendarmes on either side of him, the officer leading the way with a drawn sword,

The man was brave enough in a brute sense, and was not given to howl over his wounds. With an aching head, and weary with a night's confinement, he still held his head erect, and looked round him with a flashing eye.

The crowd gathered rapidly and when half the distance to the station had been traversed, it had grown very numerous and somewhat dangerous.

Not only were the howls and execrations deafening, but missiles were being thrown. There were cries of "Tear him to pieces!" and the quick eyes of the officers saw hands stealing towards sashes to draw the deadly knife, the common weapon of the people.

The gendarmes all wore swords, and in obedience to a sign from their chief, drew them. A wave or two drove the crowd back a few paces, but the howling became louder than ever, and the missiles more numerous.

Suddenly there was an ugly rush from the rear, and those in front, against their will, were pressed upon the gendarmes.

The swords flashed and knives glittered. Blows were exchanged, and one of the gendarmes, stabbed to the heart, fell mortally wounded.

CHAPTER XXIX.

VARSANTA IN PRISON—NOT DEAD YET—VARSANTA
MAKES HIS ATTEMPT—THE STRUGGLE IN THE
OFFICE—OVER THE PRISON WALL.

HE gendarmes became furious, and slashed out right and left, inflicting severe wounds — some of them dangerous — one fatal. In a moment, as it were, a sea of black blood had arisen; arms were bared and raised with keen - edged knives clasped in strong brown hands.

Those in the rear called on those in front to stand back and give them place.

The gendarmes fought fiercely, and the officer, the noblest of them all, forced his way like a well-driven wedge through the thiong.

Thus, step by step, with much spilling of blood, was Varsanta, the notorious brigand, borne towards the station which was to be his temporary prison.

Through all the excitement his captors never fairly lost sight of him; but had there been a chance of getting away Varsanta dared not have availed himself of it.

Once, with his manacled hands, in the power of that maddened, raving mob. he would have been torn piecemeal.

The blood of the people was up, roused by a sudden desire to destroy a notorious villain.

Their virtuous indignation was on a par with that of the ordinary English mob.

It showed that in the heart of the worst there is a latent hatred of crime.

At last they drew near the station, when the noise of the riot being heard, a number of gendarmes rushed out to aid their fellows.

Then the mob scattered and ran for their lives, pursued by the men in authority, who showed scant mercy to those they overhauled.

As usual, many who had been drawn to the spot by curiosity only suffered; and the street was strewn with men—and women, too—who had received wounds, more or less of a dangerous nature.

And Varsanta, when he was thus safe under shelter, prison though it was, felt proud of the commotion attending his arrest.

At any rate, he had not come in durance vile like a common felon.

The affair would make a sensation, and add, in its way, something to his prestige.

And now that they had got him the authorities were bent upon keeping him.

Heavy manacles were put upon his wrists, and he was placed in one of the strongest cells. Two gendarmes stood guard over the door.

Thus far he was in safe keeping.

But, as he said, he was not dead yet.

There is an old proverb that it is one thing to cage the tiger, and another thing to keep the brute secure.

Varsanta was cast into a cell in the Naples prison

—in one of the cells where King Bomba used to con-
fine his victims—and was left to meditate on his
probable fate.   The days were past for keeping any
prisoner shackled with heavy irons, as they used in
the olden time, and the hands and limbs of the
brigand were free of any such form of con-
straint.

He sat in his cell and meditated.

Not on his probable fate ; but on the possibility
of making his escape.

The cell did not of itself give much promise of
freedom.

The walls were very thick, the only window
heavily barred, and the door massive and iron-
bound, with locks and bolts outside.

Inside it was smooth and close-fitting, and about
as yielding as the wall itself.

But Varsanta did not keep his mind dwelling
upon the cell, but on those who had charge of him.

His first care would be to study the physique
of the warder who had charge of him.

The next step would be to get some notion of the
arrangements of the prison.

In the first respect he was speedily gratified.

Towards evening the warder entered the cell,
bringing in a loaf of brown bread and a pitcher of
water.

He gave the loaf to Varsanta, and placed the
pitcher on the ground, keeping his face to the
prisoner.

" This is all you will get each day," he said.   " In
a little while I will bring you a rug to sleep on, and

"No," said the warder, with a smile, "you are such a valuable dog that we shall run you out alone."

Having said this much he retreated, keeping his face to the brigand, and closed the door.

The only visible weapon he possessed was a stout staff in a case at his side, something like the truncheon of our constables at home.

"A strong man," hissed Varsanta, "and well up to his work. My only chance is to take him by surprise."

In a philosphical spirit he partook of the humble fare left by the warder, and by-and-bye, when the door was opened again, and a rug tossed in, he rolled himself up in it, stretched himself upon the floor, and fell asleep.

In the middle of the night he was awoke suddenly by a booming sound, and, springing up, listened intently. All was still.

There was not a sound within the prison walls that he could hear.

"What was it?" he muttered, and then without any definite cause he burst into a profuse perspiration, and a mortal fear fell upon him.

It lasted only a moment or two, and he was himself again.

"A blight upon it!" he muttered. "What was it, and whence did it come?"

After listening awhile and getting no solution to the cause of his sudden waking, for the stillness remained profound, he again lay down, and soon slept as soundly as before.

The next time he awoke daylight was in his cell,

The sentries were being changed, and the voice of the officer in command of the squad sounded loud and clear in the morning air.

One man was left pacing up and down near the window of his cell.

"They take good care of me," he said, grimly; "but we shall see."

Some bread and a further supply of water was brought to him by the warder with the intimation that in half an hour he would be allowed to take exercise.

Varsanta expressed his satisfaction in a courteous manner, and composedly went on with his breakfast.

In due time the cell door was thrown open, and he was bidden to come forth.

On emerging into the passage he found that a file of soldiers, in addition to the warder, was ready to accompany him.

"I feel honoured with so good an escort," he said, drily; "it is almost royal."

They did not answer, but a faint smile of approval passed across the faces of the soldiers.

They admired coolness and courage, even in a brigand.

He was escorted down a long passage to a small office, where an officer sat at a table writing.

He looked up at Varsanta, and asked if he had anything to complain of.

"Only my lack of liberty," replied the brigand chief.

"You do not need any medical attendance?"

"No."

"The prisoner may pass."

The warder opened a door on the opposite side of

the office, and Varsanta was ushered into a small court-yard.

Three sides of it were wings of the huge, sombre prison, the fourth was a high, blank wall, with some ugly-looking spikes upon the top of it.

It was the latter that was most interesting to the brigand chief, for above it was the bright blue sky, and beyond it was liberty.

No wild bird, freshly caught and caged, ever felt more deeply than Varsanta the loss of freedom. He felt as if he could rush at that wall and fight a way through it, or, failing, beat out his life by dashing his head against its pitiless stones.

But for all his agony he was prudent.

He did not seemingly take any particular notice of that wall, or exhibit any signs of restlessness.

Cool as he had been since his incarceration, he strolled round and round the yard, occasionally making some jaunty remark to his escort, which they were forbidden by the rules of the prison to answer.

"It is hard work talking for all," he said at last, "so I will be silent."

And he said no more, but went round and round, covertly seeking out some point of vantage in that high, dismal wall.

Finally, he decided that the right-hand corner was the most available place, for there the iron-work did not run quite up to the end. There was a gap of a few inches—nothing more—but in his eyes it was enough.

He knew that the iron spikes revolved, and any effort to fix a rope upon them would be futile. The slightest tug would turn them round, and then down that rope would come.

It is true he had not got a rope ; but there was a
rug which, properly torn up and twisted, could be
made into one. Whether it would be strong enough
to bear the weight of a man depended on the quality
of the material of which it was made.

They took him back to his cell, and he spent the
next hour in measuring out the rug to see if there
was enough of it. But try it which way he would,
it fell short of what he required.

What was to be done ?

He speedily hit upon a device. When the gaoler
came in later on he would get up a fictitious shiver-
ing fit, and perhaps another rug would be given
him.

The ruse succeeded. His acting was admirable,
and the warder, reporting his condition to his
superiors, another rug was given to him.

Now all that he needed was the time and opportunity to carry out his designs.

It was too late that evening, but it might be done
in the morning.

The warder came to his cell as early as six o'clock,
and then—well—he would see.

"I am not dead yet," he said, between his teeth ;
"and if I get away from here let those English dogs
look to themselves."

Patiently the brigand chief worked all the night
through, tearing up the two rugs into long strips
and twisting them into a rough semblance of a
rope.

Not once did he close his eyes, or so much as
thought of sleep, for the fever of wild hope was
upon him.

"For liberty or death !" he said a hundred times
between his teeth.

It was still dark when his work was done, and the rope, closely coiled, placed in a position to be hidden from the eyes when the door of the cell was opened by the warder.

On his success in tackling that man would lie his first chance of escape.

Ordinary weapons he did not possess, but for all that there was one to hand which might serve if he could deftly use it.

The water-pitcher was of stout stoneware, and strong, so as to bear the rough usage of prison life. A blow on the head with it, dealt by a strong arm, would scatter the wits of a man, if it did not kill him.

He emptied the water out of it, tested its weight, poised it this way and that, so as to find out the better way to use it, and when the hour for the coming of the warder drew near he was fully prepared for the attempt to be free.

Or, better still, there was the small, stout stool, given him to sit upon.

Though his blood ran like liquid fire through his veins, he was outwardly cool, and his cunning never failed him.

When at last the footsteps of the approaching warder were heard, he put the pitcher to his lips and was partaking of a sham drink, when a man with a loaf of bread under his arm entered the cell.

"What! thirsty so early my friend?" he said.

These were the last words he uttered in this world.

With a lightning-like sweep, the stool was raised, and descended upon the head of the startled man.

He fell without a groan.

Varsanta, by the sheer force of his blow, fell forward upon the rude drinking-vessel supplied to him.

The pitcher was broken, but a portion of it, with the handle attached, remained. Varsanta, stooping over the senseless man, drew his staff from the case by his side.

What recked the villain that the poor man had a wife and family who never more would hear his voice? What to him, this monster man, was the fact that in a few hours a house would be filled with weeping of mourners—a mother surrounded by her wailing children?

He could have left the man to recover from the blow, and his chance of escape be as good as it could be ; but, no, the tiger spirit was raised within him, and he must take life for the demoniacal pleasure of the awful work.

Remorselessly the fatal blows were dealt with the heavy staff, and the wild-eyed Varsanta, stained in crime from head to heel, stole out of the cell with his crude rope upon his arm.

Attached to one end of it was the broken portion of the pitcher with the handle, to serve as a weight to toss it over the wall and as something to catch hold in that narrow space between the spikes and wall in the right-hand corner.

In the corridor was another warder at the end furthest from the office. He had seen nothing, heard nothing, and was standing with his back to the brigand.

Down the passage glided Varsanta to the office. He tried the door.

It opened to his touch, and he entered it.

Only one person was there—a boy, a prisoner

even as the brigand was, engaged in cleaning it up.
The boy saw him in a moment, and stopped work,
staring at Varsanta breathlessly.

He guessed, being shrewd in the ways of criminals, what he was about to do, and true to his class,
would have done nothing to foil him in his purpose.

He said as much, but Varsanta would not trust
him.

The boy cried—

" I'll say nothing—I swear !"

And the answer was a blow from that cruel staff—
only one, but it sufficed, and yet another life was
ended.

The blood boils as one thinks of these things ; but
they have been done, and deeds much more cruel,
by men of the Varsanta type.

He cared for nothing but his personal safety, and,
without a pang, left the dead boy behind him, and
passed through the door into the exercise-yard.

All silent there—nobody about. Swiftly he
crossed the open space, coiling his rope as he went
along, and with unerring aim cast the fragment of
the pitcher over the wall just where he desired it
should be.

And now came the test of the strength of his
rope.

He tried it with two quick jerks, and, finding it
held fast, began to ascend with the skill of an acro-
bat.

The corner formed by the wall and the wing of
the building helped him, and barely a minute
elapsed ere he reached the top.

To draw up his rope and cast it down on the
other side was a matter of a few moments. Nobody
was about, save a tottering, purblind old man, wend-

ing his way to morning matins, and he had his eyes upon the ground.

Varsanta slid down recklessly and so swiftly that he heated his nether garments as if they had been held before a fierce fire.

His exhilaration had the effect of strong drink upon him.

Twice he leaped into the air, wildly tossing his arms above his head, and then he sped away, heading for the country.

Not dead yet—but free !

Once more the fiend is loose, and let all who have need to fear his cunning and cruelty be wary of him.

He vanished like some evil spirit, fleeing before the light of the morning, and barely was he out of sight when a great cry went up from the prison.

The dead had been found, and his escape discovered.

The tramping of feet and the rattle of arms were heard, and in a few minutes messengers were flying in every direction with the direful news.

But too late.

Varsanta was free, and by cunning and swiftness of foot was well away from all immediate fear of being taken again.

CHAPTER XXX.

ONCE MORE A HERO—RIBSTONE PIPPING PRE-PARES FOR EMERGENCIES.

HE has escaped—Varsanta has escaped!"

The cry rang round Naples with the speed of the electric current, and once more the fickle population raised him to the pinnacle of a hero.

That he had committed two awful crimes did not, with some, detract from his revived merits. He had outwitted the authorities, broken away from the strongest prison in Italy, and was free. But in many a feeling of fury was roused.

The news reached the hotel where our friends were staying just as Ribstone Pipping and his limited family were sitting down to breakfast.

On the valiant Pipping it had the effect of temporarily scattering his breath and taking his appetite away.

"Save us, Jane!" he said. "What next will the villain do?"

"He wants a few women to look after him," replied Mrs. Pipping, with a sharp nod of the head; "and I would like to be one of 'em."

"Jane," said Pipping, "you are a double woman—there are two of you."

"That's nonsense!" said the ever-agreeable Coriolanus.

"Eh—what's that?" exclaimed Pipping.

"I said it was nonsense," repeated Coriolanus. "How can mother be two women?"

"Look here," said Pipping, "I'm not going to argue this or any other point with you. Eat your breakfast, and don't talk."

Coriolanus snorted, and helped himself to some broiled ham.

His father helped himself also, but that was all he could do.

His appetite was gone.

"I don't think my life would be worth tuppence if I met that Varsanta," he sighed. "Heigho!"

He resolved to arm himself forthwith.

Not far from the hotel was a shop where they sold revolvers, and all sorts of weapons down to knuckle-dusters.

Thither, after a futile attempt to eat something, he wended his way.

To his great joy he found Percy Winter there examining some first-class revolvers, poising them, and testing the springs of the triggers.

"Morning, Mr. Winter," he said. "You have heard the news, I suppose?"

"I have," replied Percy; "and for the future I shall rely upon myself rather than the guardians of the law in Naples. Whenever and wherever I meet Varsanta I will shoot him like a dog!"

"Just what I've made up my mind to do," replied Pipping, airily, "and I've come to choose a tool for the job."

They spoke in English, but the shopkeeper, a dark, keen-eyed man, understood them, and smiled.

He could sum up Ribstone Pipping without any assistance.

Percy selected a pair of revolvers, and Pipping was left behind to bargain for himself.

The shopkeeper possessed a persuasive tongue, and induced him to buy so many articles of offence and defence that he left the shop a walking arsenal.

In each of his breast-pockets, outside and in, he had a loaded revolver ; in one of his tail-pockets a knuckle-duster with spikes ; in the other a short but exceedingly heavy life-preserver.

In addition to these things he had a pair of daggers, and, as a protection for himself, he had been persuaded to buy a jacket of coarse chain mail, machine-made, and put it on over his shirt.

The day was hot and oppressive. Ribstone Pipping felt like one bowed down with an unbearable burden, that could not be shaken off.

He also had the sensation of one who is in company with a dangerous explosive which may at any moment go off, and blow him goodness knows where.

He ought to have felt safe, thus heavily armed ; but he did not.

One of those revolvers might go off—the least thing would do it.

"Suppose somebody gave me a smack on the chest in a friendly way?" he thought ; "or some careless fellow ran against me? Bang would go one of them, sure as fate."

At that moment he stepped upon a piece of fruit lying upon the pavement, and down he went into a sitting position.

Oh ! that knuckle-duster and its spikes.

He writhed a moment or two, for he had sat upon that fearsome weapon, and then got upon his feet again.

" To Jericho with it !" he muttered.

Then he thought that he would change it to another pocket, and put one of the revolvers in its place.

To do this in secret he retired into a doorway, and, having in a gingerly way drawn out the firearm, was about to transfer it to his tail-pocket, when it went off.

Goodness knows how it happened, but off it went, and the bullet went slick through the door into the house.

Ribstone Pipping dropped the weapon and staggered into the street.

There he saw a number of people staring about them, uncertain of the direction from whence the sound proceeded.

He thought it advisable to clear out ; but ere he had gone far a wild-eyed man appeared in the doorway of that house, holding the revolver in his hand.

Immediately there was a little crowd round him, and this was Pipping's opportunity.

He slipped into the hotel unobserved, and took refuge in his bedroom.

" I've got another of 'e n in my pocket," he thought. " I wonder if that will go off too."

He decided to carefully remove his coat and take out the deadly weapon.

He would throw it out of the window into the waste ground behind the hotel, and if anybody found it they could do what they liked with the beastly thing.

Having spread his coat upon a box, he was so intent upon getting out the weapon that he did not hear a footstep behind him.

It was Mrs. Pipping, and she stared at him, wondering what on earth he was doing.

By slow degrees he got the weapon out of his pocket, and holding it between his finger and thumb, was making his way to the window, when "Ribby !" fell upon his ears.

"Oh ! lor'," he gasped, and down went the revolver.

The carpet was thick, and no great harm came of the fall.

Mrs. Pipping stooped and picked up the weapon.

"Jane, let it alone !   It will go off !"

"Is it loaded ?" she asked, quietly, holding the muzzle unconsciously towards him.

"For goodness sake put it down !" said Pipping, dodging about in every direction ; " it's a villainous thing."

"And may I ask what you intended to do with it ?" she asked ; "but you needn't tell me.   Oh ! you murderous villain."

"Oh ! Jane," he gasped.

"You cold-blooded villain !" continued Mrs. Pipping, "to think that you can get rid of me in that way ; but I have heard of your goings on.   A gentleman's been here this morning to say as you've insulted his wife, and he'll have your life's blood. If you want to get rid of me say so, *I* won't stand in your way.   Me and Cory can live on the pound a week my mother left me anywheres."

"Jane, don't go on in that way," said Pipping. "You are—are my own true love still.   So there's been two of 'em after me ?"

"Yes, and I've their letters in my pocket, and there they are."

Pipping, after another glance at the revolver, which his wife had thrown on the bed, took the two envelopes she held towards him, and, opening the first, found the following awful communication inside it—

"The Chevalier de Pompon will thank the Signor Pipping to name a friend so that a place of meeting may be arranged. The choice of weapons is yours."

The second letter was like unto it.

"Captain Bodabillo desires the name of a friend who will act for Mistare Pipping. Early meeting necessary."

"Well, this is a nice fix for a respectable man," he said.

"It's duels they want you to fight, isn't it?" inquired Mrs. Pipping.

"It is."

"Then, of course, you'll fight 'em."

"*Me?*" exclaimed Pipping. "ME fight a duel?"

"Certainly," said Mrs. Pipping. "You don't expect me to fight 'em for you, I hope?"

"*I* won't go into such a thing," said Pipping, angrily. "Why should I risk my life in the fool's game."

"Ribby," replied his wife, "*you've got to do it* When we come to a country like this and they give us nothing but slops and kickshaws for dinner we've got to eat 'em. If it's the rule to have duels you've got to fight 'em."

Pipping covered his face and groaned.

"What am I to fight with?" he asked. "I couldn't

hit a helephant in a month with a revolver, and, as for a sword, why, it would be no more use to me than a toothpick. But I see how it is. Jane," he added, fiercely, "you want me dead. You want *me* dead so that you can marry that Captain Boda—Boda— what the devil is his name?"

"What do you say," cried Mrs. Pipping, "you shrimp? Tell me— Take that!"

It was a fair, open-handed smack, such as might have been given with the bellows, and Pipping, reeling, fell, once more sitting upon his knuckle-duster.

Down into his pocket he thrust his hand, clean through the cloth, and in hauling out the aggravating weapon tore the lining to shreds.

He was about to dash the knuckle-duster through the window, or under the bed, anywhere out of his reach, when a thought flashed upon him.

" Ha—ha !" he cried, " I have it. The choice of weapons is mine. It shall be so. What ho ! there, knuckle-dusters for three."

" Ribby," cried his wife, in agony, " don't look like that. You are mad."

" Can you wonder at it !" he shrieked. " Look at what I've gone through with in this filthy macaroni brigand country. Mad ! Of course I am. Here, let me go and get some straw for my hair. What ho ! knuckle-dusters for three, half a gallon of arnica, and a mile of sticking-plaster !"

He dashed out of the room, and Mrs. Pipping, with a groan, sank upon a chair.

" Yes," she said ; " he's mad—stark, staring mad ! Oh ! what is that ?"

An awful crash, followed by the oaths and cries of men, uprose from the regions below. Rising with an effort she staggered towards the door, crying—

"Oh! Ribby—my—Ribby—what have you done?"

CHAPTER XXXI.

PIPPING'S MISHAP—THE GAME OF BOUNCE AS PLAYED BY THREE PEOPLE.

RS. PIPPING somehow managed to get half-way down the grand staircase, and then she saw the origin of that awful crash. Surrounded by a number of waiters and laughing guests were two men—her husband and a garcon.

Both were bespattered from head to foot with a custard-like mixture, and on the ground lay a tray and about a score of broken glasses.

The meaning of all this was clear.

In his wild, mad flight down-stairs Ribstone Pipping had encountered a garcon coming up with a tray of ices or custards, or both, and a direful collision followed.

As Pipping was talking, or rather raving, in English, and everybody else was clattering in Italian, the confusion was extreme. All talkers and no listeners seldom put right a matter in dispute.

Mrs. Pipping braced herself up, and with an appalling majesty upon her she descended the stairs. By a simple process she put an end to the scene.

"Go into the laboraterry, Ribby, and wash yourself," she said.

And as Pipping turned away the once-gentle wife fixed an eye on each of the garcons in turn, and one by one they melted away from the sunlight of her piercing glance.

Then she ascended the stairs and retired to her chamber, where, the reaction setting in, she flopped down and had a quiet faint all to herself.

In a café not far away from the hotel sat Captain Bodabillo and Chevalier de Pompon sipping weak wine and water and smoking cirgarettes.

The chevalier was the husband of the lady to whom Ribstone Pipping, in the innocence of his heart, paid some unjustifiable attention.

He was a friend of the captain's, and talking over affairs together they compared notes about Pipping, and plotted together to avenge themselves, and, if possible, make a little bit of money out of him.

In short, they were playing the game of bounce.

"He will not fight," said Bodabillo, "but will pay money."

"Good," the chevalier said in reply, "and money is better than blood."

So there they were, at the café, awaiting an answer to their respective challenges.

They had been there some time, for the reason that the delivery of the letters to Ribstone Pipping had been delayed, and there was also the mishap with the garcon to increase the lapse of time between the challenge and answer.

"He is a long time sending, this Englishman," said the chevalier.

"Ah! yes, he writes slowly," replied the captain.

"Perhaps he has run away."

"St. Joseph forbid!"

This was a horrible thought, for both the chevalier and the captain had been calculating on a good round sum from the purse of the "little fat Englishman."

But Pipping had not run away, and in a few minutes a messenger appeared with a letter for each of the expectant ones.

Captain Bodabillo tore his open, and, glancing at the contents, uttered an oath.

The chevalier did the same thing, save that his oath was a groan.

"What says he to you?" asked Bodabillo.

"He writes as follows—

"'*I will be at the waste ground behind the hotel to-morrow morning at five with the weapons ; no seconds wanted.*   "'RIBSTONE PIPPING.'"

"Word for word what he writes to me," said Bodabillo ; and then they exchanged glances of disappointment and dismay.

"Let me see," said the captain, "you challenged him first."

"No ; it was you," returned the chevalier.

"No ; *you*."

"I say YOU."

They glanced at each other and snapped their teeth, but nothing more came of it.   There was not an ounce of fight in either of them.

Presently they quieted down, and the chevalier said—

"We can object. If there are no seconds we need not fight."

"Perhaps it is the custom of his country," said Bodabillo, doubtfully.

"A fig for his country!"

"Ah! but he will call us cowards."

"He will never dare."

"He will.　If he means to fight he will stick at nothing.　None of these English ever do."

"I have it," said the chevalier; "the fool has asked us *both* to meet him.　There will be no seconds —no witnesses.　We can both—"

"Hush !" interposed Bodabillo, looking hurriedly around him, "do not let anybody hear.　It is a good thought.　We will both go, and for the honour of our native land we will punish this audacious foreigner."

"We will."

"Chevalier, I drink to you !"

"Captain, to you !"

It was an oversight on the part of Ribstone Pipping to appoint the same hour for both meetings; but having done it, he meant to go through the business.

His wife promised to get him ready for the event by stimulating him with a little sal volatile, of which dangerous extract she admitted occasionally taking a drop herself.

Moreover, she would witness the encounter from behind the curtain of the bedroom, and Pipping, thus doubly strengthened, felt that he could, as he said, "go in and win."

He bought an extra pair of knuckle-dusters, so as to have everything fair, and at an early hour retired to rest.

He felt very much like a man about to be executed; but, like many notorious criminals on the eve of going to the scaffold, he slept.

Mrs. Pipping took good care not to oversleep herself, and awoke her spouse at four o'clock.

"Get up, Ribby," she said; "it's a lovely morning."

"I'm glad of that," he said, wretchedly. "I sup-pose they haven't come yet?"

"Not they!"

He got out of bed and dressed himself, and when it wanted ten minutes to the time Mrs. Pipping poured him out a strong dose of sal volatile, which he drank off It made him gasp for breath, and ran through his veins like the electric current.

He became as bold as brass.

"I'll give 'em both something," he said, "for the glory of old England!"

"Remember, Ribby," said Mrs. Pipping, "that my eye is on you. If you cave in to these trumpery foreigners I will give it to you."

"I'll give 'em beans!" he said.

He went downstairs and out of the hotel by a back door. Nobody as yet was stirring, and there was not so much as a tom-cat outside to witness the deadly fray.

Almost at the same moment the gallant captain and the fire-eating chevalier appeared upon the ground. Bows were exchanged.

"You have brought the weapons with you?" said the captain.

"I have 'em here," replied Pipping, producing his knuckle-dusters; "there's one each for you and two for me. I'll fight the pair at once, and get it over."

He slipped his on, and gave them one each.

They looked at them wonderingly, and with a tendency to sink into their boots.

"On with 'em and stand up," said Pipping.

They did not readily obey, and he was impatient. He made a few passes at them, and then, before either knew the full purport of his movements, he dealt each a blow, one on the nose and the other just under the ear.

They went down as if they had been shot upon the battle-field, and lay quite still.

Pipping bent down and stared at their still faces and staring eyes.

"Good Heavens !" he exclaimed, " I've killed 'em both."

And now himself well scared, he darted back into the hotel.

Mrs. Pipping gave her husband a right royal welcome on his return to her.

"Billy," she said, "you are a brave man. I didn't think it was in you."

"I am, my love," he said. "If you are summoned to the inquest don't you say a word about your husband's share in this business."

"Not me," she said. "Let them Italians make what they can of it."

"I wonder how the—the corpses are getting on !" said Pipping, after a few moments' silence.

CHAPTER XXXII.

PURSUING THE BRIGAND—RIBSTONE PIPPING MAKES ONE OF THE SEARCH PARTY.

BOTH Mr. and Mrs. Pipping were in a very anxious state, in spite of their sense of triumph. In an hour or so the dark deed would be discovered, and then would come the commotion.

"Jane," said Pipping, "have a peep at 'em, will you?"

"You do it," she said.

"Suppose we do it together?"

"Ah! that's the thing."

So they stood up to the window together and beheld the two corpses on their feet, each holding his face, and evidently exchanging comments on their recent encounter.

"Why, Ribby," said Mrs. Pipping, in a disappointed tone, "you ain't killed 'em after all."

"Not quite, it seems," he replied.

"Well! wouldn't it be right to go down again and settle 'em?"

"Jane, you ask too much. Let 'em go. It wouldn't be fair to kill 'em twice in one day."

In a few moments Captain Bodabillo and the Chevalier de Pompon walked slowly away, stopping every few steps to feel their jaws. If not killed outright they had received something they would not easily forget.

Ribstone Pipping carefully and tenderly wrapped up the knuckle-dusters wherewith he had done such good work, and then lay down on the bed in his clothes to await the ringing of the breakfast bell.

It seemed a long time coming, but it came at last, and having given a few touches to their toilets husband and wife went downstairs.

More news of Varsanta. Waiters and everybody full of the story of his escape from prison.

The whole of the gendarmes in the city were on the alert seeking him in every possible place, routing out the poorer and more dangerous districts and bringing to light much that was unnecessary in the form of depraved and criminal humanity.

Expeditions were all being formed to scour the country round, for the last two ghastly crimes of the now trebly notorious brigand had roused the entire population.

On emerging Pipping learnt that Percy Winter and Will Gordon had partaken of breakfast, and gone forth to lend their aid in the search.

"Why on earth didn't they tell me they were going?" indignantly demanded Pipping.

"The signor is out too late," said one of the waiters, politely. "Other parties are being formed. Varsanta is to be secured."

"Ribby," said Mrs. Pipping, "you ought to go."

Ribby would rather have remained at home, but he had committed himself by his feigned indignation, and could not draw back.

"As soon as I've had breakfast," he said, "I shall be ready."

Coriolanus, who had overslept himself, was crawl-

ing into the breakfast-room, looking sullen and
heavy-eyed.

"Of course you've breakfasted!" he said. "Why
didn't you call me?"

"Ribby," said Mrs. Pipping, "that boy wants
more drilling than we've given him. You've spoilt
him."

"I'll spoil him!" said Pipping, between his teeth.
"Boy, peg away at your breakfast. You are going
out with me."

Coriolanus muttered something under his breath,
but he ate his breakfast, and did not demur to the
proposed trip—simply because he had no idea of
the nature of it.

Shortly after this Pipping received an intimation
that a party, headed by gendarme, would be at the
door in half-an-hour. He could join it if he
desired.

"Rib," again said Mrs. Pipping, "you've got to
go."

"All right," he answered, recklessly. "I don't
care. I'll go upstairs and get ready."

He departed forthwith, and when he came back
he walked in a stiff-necked way, and his pockets
were bulky.

Coriolanus was ready by that time, and, quite unconscious of the true nature of the expedition,
cheerfully got ready to start.

Outside, a dozen men in a brake were waiting.
They were commanded by a fierce-looking man in
some sort of uniform, the chief feature of which
was an enormous cocked hat.

Mrs. Pipping, with two or three waiters behind
her, came out to see her husband off.

At the bottom of the hotel steps she threw her

arms around him, but immediately relaxed her hold, and stared him full in the face.

"Ribby!" she exclaimed, "what—"

"Oh! it's all right.   Don't you bother," he said, hurriedly.   "Where's that boy?"

Coriolanus, with his usual affectionate courtesy, had got into the trap without a word of adieu to his mother.

As she looked at him tenderly he gave her back a sulky nod.

"You'd better say Good-bye to your mother," said Ribstone Pipping.

"Oh! don't worry me," growled Coriolanus.

His mother turned away and hurried up the hotel steps with tears in her eyes.

Bad as he always behaved to her he was her son.

"He wants something to make him *think*," she said.

Little did she fancy how soon he would get that something, and what would be the effect upon him.

Ribstone Pipping had a seat offered him by the side of the man with the cocked hat, and the brake started.

A small knot of people which had collected outside the hotel cried, "Brava!" and clapped their hands.   Pipping's heart warmed up a little, and he felt for the moment like a hero.

Then he thought of his wife, and a grim smile spread over his face.

"She felt IT," he said, softly, and then he chuckled.

What "it" was we shall presently find out.

The brake bore away out of the town, in the direction of Herculaneum and Pompei.

For Italy, the horses were extremely good, and carried them along at a smart pace.

The man in the cocked hat was disposed to be friendly; but his stock of English was limited to "rosbif," a word beginning with a big D, and "Portare-beere," so the exchange of ideas was not very great.

On their way they stopped twice to refresh at a roadside wineshop, and some of the party got very bold indeed.

They expressed their sorrow that Varsanta had not met them when alone, so that they might individually have had the glory of capturing him; but that sort of thing wore off with the wine.

When they reached Herculaneum a curious, damp sort of silence had fallen upon the party.

Then they deserted the brake and took to some mules which were in waiting.

Ribstone Pipping and the man in the cocked hat headed the cavalcade, and close behind them was Coriolanus.

"I say, father," he said, "ain't we going a long way. We sha'n't be home for dinner."

"Some of us may not," replied Pipping, drily. "Get up—you ugly brute."

He dug his heels into the sides of his mule, which had shown a strong disposition to lag, and they trotted on for a mile or so, up the sloping ground, until they came to a little village nestling on the side of Vesuvius.

Above them, sloping upward as it seemed to the very sky, was grim, sulky, destructive Vesuvius.

From her crown arose the column of smoke which had been noticeable for days; but now its action was varied.

Every now and then the smoke would suddenly increase in density, and then die away almost to nothing.

After that it would slowly resume its original appearance.

There was only spasmodic talking among the men now, and as they spoke in Italian, Ribstone Pipping did not understand them.

But he observed that they always, when addressing each other, raised their eyes to that smoking crown.

"They make a lot o' fuss about their mountain," muttered Pipping; "but I don't see much in it."

He and Coriolanus had said very little to each other on the way, but soon that very unamiable youth began to resent the length of the journey.

"I've had enough of this, father," he said, more than once.

To which Ribstone Pipping responded—

"If you want to go back you can go alone."

At last Coriolanus said he would go, and was pulling the head of his mule round, when his father checked him by saying—

"Cory, it ain't safe for you to do it."

"Not safe!" exclaimed the boy.

"No; we've come here after that Varsanta the brigand, and he might be skulking around, you know."

The cheeks of Coriolanus became of a dull lead colour, and his hands shook so that he almost dropped the reins.

"You ought to have left me at home. It isn't fair!" he whined.

"I don't see why we should consider you," *replied*

his father ; "you never considered your mother or me."

"But I may be killed, father !"

"So may I, Cory."

Ribstone Pipping spoke with all seriousness. He was almost as solemn as the Italians, who were now preternaturally grave.

That their course had been arranged was clear, for every now and then the man in the cocked hat stopped to look about him and study the bearings of the country, and after awhile he made Pipping understand by signs that other parties went out that morning, bearing upwards to the cone from different points.

———

CHAPTER XXXIII.

THE BRIGAND ON THE MOUNTAIN—PIPPING IN PURSUIT—SURELY THIS IS THE END?

DOTTED about the sides of the great mountain, half way up the sides, are Italian villages, where the shepherds who look after the flocks of goats and the labourers in the vineyards live.

One of these places is named Felugia, a collection of about fifty peasant homes, somewhat scattered, and a single wineshop.

It was here, on the morning of the day on which we are dwelling, that a gendarme appeared in a breathless condition with the startling announcement—

"Varsanta the brigand is loose, and is on the mountain. Keep close. Band yourselves together, and if he appears capture him."

Then the gendarme hurried on to carry the tidings elsewhere, and the terrified peasants called a council among themselves.

It was speedily settled that they would not, for that at day least, scatter themselves about the vineyards, but keep together, and, if the brigand appeared, give him a warm reception.

But it is one thing to talk and another to act.

Within an hour of the arrival and departure of the gendarme, Varsanta himself appeared.

Alone he came boldly into the village and found it apparently deserted.

He had been seen approaching, and although not personally known, save by name, his identity was guessed at, and the inhabitants promptly hid themselves in their houses and other convenient places.

Varsanta was hungry and thirsty. He also limped a little, for he had travelled far and was footsore.

Possibly he understood the deserted appearance of the village, for there was a smile on his face as he walked, with as much swagger as he could assume, in the direction of the wineshop.

The door was open, but the place was deserted.

Landlord and family had hidden away, and were trembling like scared rats in the cellar.

The story of Varsanta's cruel murders in the

prison, and other atrocities he had committed, had reached them.

Quite at his ease, or apparently so, the brigand entered the bar, and seizing a bottle of wine emptied it at a draught.

After that he regaled himself with the only food he could find—coarse, black bread and goat's-milk cheese.

"I suppose there is nothing to pay?" he said, with a laugh; "and if there was, I haven't a stiver about me. Like other gentlemen in trouble, I must now live upon credit."

He searched a drawer in the bar with the hope of finding some money, but there was none.

All he discovered was a big, keen-edged knife, which he took possession of.

"I may want you, my friend," he said.

Having put a flask of wine into one pocket, and some bread and cheese into another, he left the inn and renewed his ascent up the mountain.

On a knoll outside the village he stopped to take a downward glance, and from his elevated post he could see three collections of black dots moving up towards him.

"If I could only see a place to hide in, and double on them like a fox?" he muttered.

But such places are not easy to find upon Vesuvius, for it is essentially a tremendous hill of lava, fairly smooth on the upper half, and lacking the jaggedness of ordinary mountains.

Still, it is broken up here and there right away to the summit, and the brigand had hopes of finding some burrow in which he could lie close until his pursuers had passed, and then double back and find a safe hiding place.

By some means the authorities had got a very clear idea of his movements, and the pursuit was very keen.

From every side search parties were approaching, and only two things remained for him to do. He must either play cunning, or boldly cut his way through the bands of pursuers.

The latter was more to his taste just then, for he felt very much like a hunted wolf, and the fighting humour was very strong upon him.

He threw himself down beside a knoll to rest. He had need of it, for he had travelled all night on foot, and now his iron constitution had to yield to fatigue.

It was not his intention to sleep, but the feeling came on so suddenly that he could not resist. Unconsciousness descended upon him like a cloud.

For hours he laid there wrapped in slumber—unheeded and alone.

Then suddenly, as if shaken by a rude hand, he awoke with a start.

For a moment he stared at the sky above his head in a state of semi-bewilderment.

Then a voice fell upon his ear—a familiar voice.

"I don't think it's any use going any further. He isn't up here. Why don't you go back?"

An answer was given in Italian, and Varstone, who understood both languages, grasped the fact that neither speaker understood the other.

It was a case of mutual reproach.

Both wanted to return, but neither liked to set the example, thinking that the other wanted to go on.

The brigand laughed and took out from his pocket the knife he had stolen from the inn

With a lightning sweep the stool descended on the head of the startled man.

"A pair of curs !" he muttered. "I'll settle them if only for the sport of it."

But his quick ear soon detected that there were more than two footsteps, and peering over the knoll he saw a straggling party of nearly a dozen.

In the van was Ribstone Pipping and the man wearing the cocked hat.

Straggling behind were the other men, and, last of all, young Coriolanus, tearful and trembling.

"And they have been fools enough to send this crew against ME," muttered Varsanta. "Why, a snap of my finger would scare them all."

Refreshed by his long sleep, and in the humour for the shedding of blood, he crouched behind the knoll, waiting, knife in hand, for his prey.

On came the unconscious and unwilling leaders of the parties, each confounding the other for his persistence in the pursuit, until there was only a few feet between them and their skulking foe.

Then suddenly up sprang Varsanta and dashed at them.

A yell burst from the lips of the man in the cocked hat, and wheeling round, he ran down the mountain side, upsetting two of his followers in the rush.

Others followed his example, and young Coriolanus, sulkily meditating as he tramped along, was bowled over and sent to the ground with sufficient force to scatter his wits.

For a moment or two he heard the noise of rushing water in his ears, and a hundred fires danced before his eyes. After this came the darkness of insensibility.

Meanwhile, all the Italians had fled down the side of the mountain, and only Ribstone Pipping remained to do battle with Varsanta.

And his staying was against his will, the fact being he was too terrified to stir.

"Ah! you Pi—ping," said Varsanta, between his teeth; "you com—ic, funnee man. So I have you."

In a feeble way Ribstone Pipping felt in his pockets for his knuckle-duster, which, in a dim way, he knew to be there.

But beyond touching it with his fingers he did nothing.

"Come here!" cried Varsanta, seizing him by the collar! "Get ready to DIE. Know you not I am called *butchare*. Ah! I butchare you. Here is ze block."

He dashed the unresisting Pipping on his back and aimed a blow at him; then, changing his mind, he turned him over, face downwards, on a big stone, and, pressing one knee into his back, raised his hand with the knife in the air.

"Death—death to you!" he hissed, and, aiming at that fatal spot—the upper part of the back between the shoulder blades—he brought the weapon down with tremendous force.

His aim was true. It struck the chosen spot and —broke off short near the handle.

CHAPTER XXXIV.

VARSANTA'S AMAZEMENT—A TIMELY APPROACH.

VARSANTA let go of Ribstone Pipping, and that worthy man immediately sprang up and fled down the side of the mountain at a pace that would have resulted in a broken neck in case of a fall.

"It is a good suit of chain-mail. Hurrah!" he gasped.

Blind to all things but his personal safety, he did not notice that the prostrate form he bounded over was that of his son, but fled on and on, keeping his feet by a miracle, and so vanished from sight.

Varsanta stood still for fully half a minute staring at the shattered knife. Then he turned his eyes to the piece of blade that was upon the ground.

The point had been broken off by the force of the blow. The temper of that weapon was all that could be desired.

"What sort of man is he?" muttered Varsanta. "The knife ought to have gone through and through him!"

He shivered with affright, for there was something uncanny in the marvellous escape of the man.

And it seemed as if the mountain was moved also, for a faint trembling of the earth was felt by the brigand.

He cast a quick glance at the mountain-top.

A thin line of smoke was rising in the still air, straight as a well-built column of stone.

"Is the old girl going to wake up?" muttered the brigand. "If so, this is no place for me."

He cast away the handle of the knife, and began slowly to descend the mountain ; but he was only half way towards young Coriolanus when a cry of exultation fell upon his ears.

It came from the left, a little way down, and it arose from one of another party advancing in pursuit of him.

And present in that party were two whom the brigand bitterly hated—Percy Winter and Will Gordon.

They knew him, and he knew them, and just for

one instant the brigand felt as if his heart had ceased to beat.

Then the old bravado reasserted itself, and, taking off his hat, he bowed as if they were his dearest friends.

A good two hundred yards was between them, and, as none of the party were armed with rifles, Varsanta was for the moment safe.

But it was impossible for him to retreat down the mountain.   In that direction lay capture or death.

His one chance was to retreat up towards the cone, and dodge about until darkness came to his rescue.

Under its cover he might be able to elude them.

Always a hardy mountaineer, he was better at uphill work than those behind him, although Percy and Will were nearly as good.

They, too, had had plenty of climbing experience, and as Varsanta bounded up the sloping way, they followed in hot pursuit.

In two minutes the party of men with them, numbering half a score, were fast being left behind.

"Percy," said Will, speaking quickly in the short, sharp way of those who are half-breathed by running, "we must not lose sight of him again."

"No," was the simple answer.

After that they said no more, but with close-set teeth and a fixed look in their eyes they kept on.

But one cannot run uphill—a steep slope—long, and soon both pursued and pursuers had to slacken their pace.

All were panting and doing their best to get back that useful form of breath to the athlete—the second wind. Below, too far down to be of service, the rest of the party were toiling upward.

It was evening now, and there was a stillness in the air which, like some stages of darkness, might be felt.

It was a stillness passing that generally experienced on either land or sea.

It seemed as if the very sun had ceased its downward way to the west.

Not a bird in the air or a cloud broke the even arch of sky overhead.

Nay, more ; the column of smoke rising from Vesuvius rose so evenly that it had the appearance of a thing built and fixed, and the spreading out of its crown was imperceptible.

Every time the feet of the three men struck the lava ground a faint echo was heard aloft, unnatural and awe-inspiring.

Then suddenly the silence was broken.

From somewhere in the bowels of the mountain came a muffled roar like that of a gigantic lion in its rage.

It died away, and once more there was stillness.

Percy and Will exchanged glances, which showed that they knew what that sound portended.

But they also knew that such roaring sounds were often heard and nothing came of them.

But if the time for the rending aside of the mountain had come they would not have turned back while Varsanta kept on.

He must have no chance of escape as far as they were concerned.

As for the brigand, he, too, knew the portent of that sound, but he could not stop awhile.

He must go on—tire those Englishmen out, if he could, and so evade them.

Would the night were there !

It would not be long in coming, for the sun was almost down.

The rim of that huge luminary was kissing the horizon.

In three minutes it would be gone.

After that a short twilight and then darkness.

" Come soon, and come for ever, if you like," was the impious wish of Varsanta.

He could breathe freely again, and was hurrying on.

His pursuers, similarly favoured, were once more taking step for step with him.

But they could not gain upon the agile villain.

And now, as the sun was on the point of dipping, a strange thing happened on the summit of the mountain. The smoke suddenly stopped issuing from the crater. High above was a broken black column in the air.

Between it and the summit of the mountain was a gap of clear blue sky.

Thus volcanic matters remained for awhile. The sun disappeared, and the next moment, as if the mountain kept its own sunset gun, a shot was fired from the crater.

The boom of it was heard many a mile away, and the shot it fired was a huge stone, tons in weight, which went far up skyward, and then burst asunder like a bombshell.

Varsanta stopped and looked around him like a frightened beast.

Percy and Will stopped too, and who can wonder, for they were within measurable distance of the huge mouth which has so often spat out fire and ashes, spreading destruction, misery, and death far and wide.

And thus matters were when a sudden darkn fell upon the scene.

The sun was down, Vesuvius was still, and overhead was a huge canopy of smoke, obscuring the stars.

Darkness on all, so deep, so terrible, that Percy and Will, although but a few feet apart, could not see each other.

They stopped dead, and for a few moments uttered not a word. It was broken by a faint scratching sound, high overhead.

Varsanta was still urging his way upward, hoping to escape his pursuers.

"Is it any use to go on?" asked Will.

"I fear not," replied Percy; "we must be near the summit now."

"Within two hundred feet of the edge of the crater."

"It looks like shirking the job to go back."

"Then let us go on."

But ere they could take a step further a sensation of the mountain slowly rising came over them. They staggered and fell upon their hands and knees.

Then the silence was broken by a volume of dumb roaring down in the bowels of the earth.

"Back!" cried Percy, hoarsely; "an eruption is about to take place."

It is more than man can do to stand defiant in the presence of the awful phenomena of a volcanic erruption.

Standing in the presence of the terrible exhibition of force, but one idea remains in the human head, and that is—flight.

Before the two friends could avail themselves of __

the natural prompting a vivid flame of light shot out of the crater, casting a weird awful light upon the cloud of smoke above.

Over both of them came a feeling of the vastness and strength of created things andthey involuntarily doffed their hats.

And on the verge of the crater stood the form of a man—Varsanta.

They saw him there, upright for a moment, and then fall forwards or backwards. They could not tell which.

The flame died away and once more there was darkness.

But only for a moment.

Once more the rumbling was heard, and then one of the most terrific explosions that ever fell upon mortal ears.

A solid column of fire, laden with huge stones, leapt high into the air, the mouth of the crater parted in half-a-dozen places, and huge streams of boiling lava bubbled up and ran over.

All around was now as light as day, although it was not the light of the blessed sun, but of the infernal regions.

Will and Percy fled down the mountain side.

It was now a race between them and the lava; the stake, their lives.

Good fortune led them to the very spot where Coriolanus had been recently lying insensible.

CHAPTER XXXV.

A TERRIBLE LIGHT ON DARKNESS—THE GREAT LAVA STREAM—VARSANTA'S DOOM.

ORIOLANUS PIPPING had now recovered consciousness and was standing up, gazing about him in utter bewilderment.

Percy saw him first and recognised him.

It was not the time to stop and ask questions, and if he had done so his voice would not have been heard.

The roar of the eruption was incessant and deafening. Stones were falling about them, hot ashes fell like snow.

Seizing Coriolanus by the collar, Percy turned him round and pushed him forward.

" Fly for your life !" he cried.

The words were unheard, but the action sufficed. Coriolanus, with a wild terror upon him, ran with them down the mountain side.

How they kept their feet was a marvel, a mystery which they could never afterwards explain.

Boom !

An explosion within the volcano of such awful force that it seemed as if the earth had been rent asunder.

They had reached a part of the mountain which was comparatively level for fifty yards or thereabouts.

Instinctively they slackened their speed, and looked around.

What an awful sight met their view !

The sky above the mountain was a huge mass of fire, and over the crater lip the lava poured like a cataract. The whole crown of the mountain was red hot.

And the deadly stream was not far behind them.

One moment they stared at it awe-stricken, and then Percy clasped Will by the arm, pointing at the edge of the advancing lava-stream.

Near it was the form of a man—Varsanta !

He was not running as they had been, but staggering along with his two hands to his head, and the light was so strong that they could see a stream of blood running down his face.

He had been struck on the head by one of the stones which were now literally raining down.

Great as their peril was, Will and Percy felt impelled to watch the movements of the doomed man.

Beside them stood Coriolanus, his hands over his face, and screaming like a frightened child.

But they could not hear, and were too absorbed in watching Varsanta to heed him.

Not for long was their watching.

With dreadful swiftness the red-hot lava gained upon the lost man.

In vain he staggered on, with his wild eyes moving to and fro, in the hopeless manner of a stag with a pack of fierce hounds at its heels.

The lava swept upon him and caught his feet.

He sank upon his knees.

Oh ! horror.

Whatever the man might have done in his life, his death was too awful to look upon, save with a feeling of pity.

They saw him, deep in the burning liquid, battle furiously with his clenched fists, and then fall forward on his hands.

Even now his head moved about in agony, but all was soon over. A wave of lava came down and swept over him.

Varsanta the brigand was gone, and no mortal man would ever set eye on him again.

In a few minutes not even his ashes would be distinguishable. He was destroyed, obliterated, wiped out of existence.

It made the observers reel, but, recovering, they each took an arm of the dazed Coriolanus, and half led, half dragged him down the mountain side.

And now the volcano was in full activity.

Great billows of lava were rolling down its side, faster and faster.

He, who being near it, would escape, must run swiftly.

On—on Percy and Will, and trip not. A heavy fall would be fatal.

They could feel the heat of that awful stream, and every few moments some huge stone would fall near them, striking the earth with a force which left no doubt as to their fate if one should fall upon them.

On—on, for their lives, sped the friends, holding up the poor-hearted, bewildered Coriolanus, on whom lay a mortal terror which is worse than any

CHAPTER XXXVI.

THE CURTAIN.

STANDING outside one of the hostelries erected near Herculaneum for the accommodation of tourists, was a group of men.

Some of them had recently been attached to parties sent in pursuit of Varsanta, and had retreated with all speed when the signs of an eruption had become unmistakable.

The hour was early morning, and the eruption had been in full play for six hours.

Happily, terrific as it was, it had not the awful force of that great outburst of eighteen hundred years ago, when Herculaneum and Pompeii were buried under the fearful storm of ashes ; but it had already overwhelmed some of the villages up the mountain side.

A number of the inhabitants, with their wives and children, and such few household goods as they could save, had struggled in, and others were on their way.

There was ruin and terror all through the district.

Among the group were two men—Ribstone Pipping and his companion of the day before—the man in the cocked hat.

By great exertion they had got thus far and safe, but Ribstone Pipping did not rejoice.

When too late he had discovered the absence of his son Coriolanus, whom he believed to be lost.

"The boy is dead," he kept on saying, "and I can never look his mother in the face again."

Then again he would cry—

"She wanted him to have a lesson to make a better boy of him—so did I. He's had his lesson, and he's made an angel of. We shall never see him again."

His wails and his tears were not much heeded by those about him.

There were other people in trouble who had need of sympathy and it was also hard to keep one's eyes off the crown of that fiery mountain.

How poor and insignificant were all the pyrotechnic displays of man in comparison !

In addition to the people flying before the eruption others were coming from Naples to get a nearer view of the scene.

Every few minutes some vehicle arrived laden with sight-seers, more or less interested in the scene.

At last one arrived with a single occupant inside —a lady—Mrs. Pipping.

She was in a violently agitated state, and as the carriage stopped outside the hostelry she hurriedly descended and cast her eyes around him.

"Has anybody seen my husband and son?" she cried.

Nobody answered her, or indeed paid much heed to her words.

The majority did not understand her, but there was one on whom her words fell like so many heavy blows.

That was Ribstone Pipping, whose first impulse

was to run away rather than face the mother who had lost her son.

But a better and more manly feeling prevailed. He had not himself to consider, but her.

She must be told the worst, and he must do his best to support her in the hour of trial.

There was not much demonstration in the way he came up to her, and holding out both hands said—

" I am here, Jane."

A cry of joy burst from her lips, and, throwing her arms about him, she held him tight.

"Oh ! Ribby," she sobbed, " I am glad to see you. And our boy—he's here, I suppose ?"

" No," hastily answered Pipping.

She released herself from him, and, drawing back, looked at him wildly.

"Don't tell me—not dead ?" she said with a wail.

"We lost him on the mountain," replied Pipping, hanging his head. " You know what a boy he was ? Poor fellow ! he would have his own way. It was no use my asking him to keep near me."

"Ribby," said Mrs. Pipping, in a low tone " I won't blame you ; but it can't be, you know. He isn't dead ?"

" I am afraid, Jane, we—we have lost him."

"He wasn't the best of sons in some things," moaned the mother ; "but he was our only child."

"We made him what he was," said Pipping ; " it was our own fault. We spoilt him."

" *I* did, Ribby, not you."

" No, it was me."

And so they went on bewailing their loss, and

reproaching themselves, almost unheeded by those around them.

By-and-bye Pipping went into the hostelry to get his wife some wine. As he was bringing it out he heard her scream.

Dropping the glass, he dashed in the direction of the cry, prepared to do any amount of damage to anyone who might be injuring her.

He saw a ring of spectators, which he broke through with scant ceremony, and came upon a spectacle that utterly staggered him.

Clasped in his mother's arms was the lost Corio-lanus, and, standing just behind the pair, were Percy Winter and Will Gordon.

The latter, seeing Ribstone Pipping, came up to him.

"We found the boy on the mountain," he said, "and helped him here. The last few miles he has had a lift in a peasant's cart."

"I can't say much now," said Pipping, passing a hand across his eyes, "but I feel that I owe you two brave fellows more than I can ever repay."

At that moment Coriolanus, gently detaching himself from his mother, came on to his father, and put his arms about him.

"I am sorry that I've been such an ungrateful cub to you," he said; "but I'll never be so any more. I feel as if I'd come back from the *grave*, and I'll keep my word."

"My boy," said Pipping, "there's no more to be said. Let the past go, and let us live for the future."

. . . .

With Varsanta dead, there came a feeling of security over the law-abiding people. The minor brigands were not considered of much account, and their trial excited very little attention.

Signor Silvio de Lustra and Aura had already sailed for England, but the rest could not go until the prisoners were disposed of.

Short was their trial, and sharp the sentence. One and all were condemned to imprisonment for life.

This business over Percy and Will set their faces towards England ; and the Pippings, having had enough of travel, wended their way thither.

In three days they were in England, and as their ways in life were somewhat different, Percy and Will parted with the others after exchanging expressions of good will.

" I've got a nice little place at Balham," said Pipping, at parting ; " Mowbray Villa—I made my money out of pies, you know. If ever you come that way, drop in."

They promised to do so, and, with a final shake of the hand, parted.

It may here be announced that Coriolanus was truly a changed boy. That night in the mountain did him good, and instead of being peevish, discontented, and worrying, he is now quiet, good-humoured, and unselfish.

Being such a comfort to his loving parents they are perfectly happy.

It will be pretty clear to the general reader that Will and Aura had made up their minds to love each other, and be true to the end, and all that sort of thing, and as soon as he had settled in town, Will set to work making the most of the talent he was endowed with.

He had a presentiment he would make *his mark,*

and did so. In a year or so he and Aura were married.

As for Percy, he, as we know, was rich and had no difficulty in getting a wife to suit him.

He found exactly what he wanted in a Scotch lassie of the good old MacDonald family, whom he met when mooning about in the Trossacks.

In deference to her he took a house near Loch Lomond, and there they spend the summer.

Will and his wife also visit them, and a very nice time they have of it all round.

Their winters are spent in England, dividing the time between the attractions of town and the delights of Percy's country house in Kent.

Thus, while knavery suffered an awful punishment, bravery meets with its just reward.

THE END.

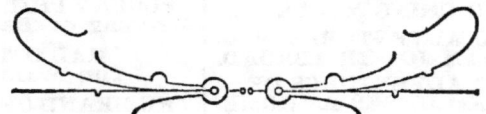

Printed by

SULLY & FORD,

1 & 30, Plough Court, Fetter Lane,

Fleet Street, E.C.

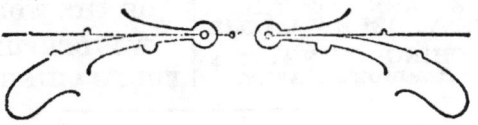

ALL VOLUMES ARE IN STOCK.

THREEPENNY COMPLETE VOLUMES.

DARING DAVE;
OR, THE TREASURES OF THE DEEP.

THE BRIGANDS OF PALESTRA.

A BOY OF A THOUSAND.

FOOTBALL IN COKETOWN; OR,
WHO SHALL BE CAPTAIN?

THE CHING CHING MYSTERY.

THE WILD ADVENTURES OF
EDDARD & JAM JOSSER ABROAD.

THE WILD ADVENTURES OF
EDDARD & JAM JOSSER AT HOME.

THE FURTHER EXPLOITS
OF EDDARD AND JAM JOSSER.

THE SLAPCRASH BOYS;
THE LIVELIEST OF SCHOOL STORIES.

JACK CŒUR DE LION:
OUTCAST AND HERO.

MAJOR NIGHTMARE OF CAMP
CLIMAX.

THE MESMERIST DETECTIVE;
OR, STRANGE DOINGS IN LITTLEWOOD.

PLUCKY PHIL FARREN; OR, THE
MYSTERY OF BRYTHEWAITE SCHOOL.

HAL O' THE HEATH,
THE WANDERING HEIR.

THE BRAND OF THE BLACK STAR.

LIONEL THE BOLD;   OR, THE
CIRCUS RIDER'S REVENGE.

VALIANT ROY; OR, THE PIRATE'S
SCOURGE.

SIXPENNY COMPLETE VOLUMES.

JACK JAUNTY,
THE HERO OF SEAGULL CLIFF.

DAUNTLESS DONALD DREW; OR,
BESET BY BITTER FOES.

RADDLETON ROCKET'S ROVING
SCHOOLBOYS.

THE ADVENTURES OF
BOLD BEN BRIERTON AND TINY
TIMOTHY TOPPEM.

OUR BOYS ABROAD;
OR, THE BLACK BANDITS OF THE
RHINE

CHING CHING AND HIS CHUMS;
A MIRTHFUL, MOVING, AND
MYSTERIOUS STORY.

JACK OF THE GOLDEN BELT;
OR, STIRRING ADVENTURES IN THE
SWAMPS OF CUBA.

YOUNG CHING AT SCHOOL;
OR, HIGH OLD TIMES FOR THE
SLAPCRASHERS.

DARING CHING CHING;
OR, THE MYSTERIOUS CRUISE OF THE
SWALLOW.

GALLANT HAL AND THE CREW
OF THE SILVER STAR.

THE VEILED CAPTAIN;
OR, THE HERO OF EAGLE CRAIG.

DICK STORNAWAY;
OR, A HERO IN SPITE OF HIS FOES.

THE BANGWELL BOYS.

ONE SHILLING COMPLETE VOLUMES.

HARDIBOY JAMES;
OR, CHUMS AND CHAPPIES.

HANDSOME HARRY OF THE
FIGHTING BELVEDERE. Vols. I. & II.

CHEERFUL CHING CHING; THE
SEQUEL TO "HANDSOME HARRY."

TOM TARTAR AT SCHOOL. Vols. I. & II.

DICK STRONGBOW, THE WONDER
OF THE WORLD. Vols. I. & II.

WONDERFUL CHING CHING.

YOUNG CHING CHING   Vols. I. & II.

TWO SHILLING COMPLETE VOLUMES.

DICK STRONGBOW, THE WONDER OF THE WORLD.

YOUNG CHING CHING.   TOM TARTAR AT SCHOOL.

HANDSOME HARRY OF THE FIGHTING BELVEDERE.

'BEST FOR BOYS' PUBLISHING CO., 17, GOUGH SQUARE, FLEET-ST., LONDON,

www.ingramcontent.com/pod-product-compliance
Lightning Source LLC
Chambersburg PA
CBHW080822250626
47160CB00008B/2829